MARCHING SEASON

Rosemary Jenkinson

MARCHING SEASON

Illustrated by Denise Jenkinson

ARLEN
HOUSE

Marching Season

is published in 2022 by

ARLEN HOUSE
42 Grange Abbey Road
Baldoyle, Dublin 13
Phone: 00 353 86 8360236
arlenhouse@gmail.com
arlenhouse.ie

978–1–85132–227–5, *paperback*

Distributed internationally by
SYRACUSE UNIVERSITY PRESS
621 Skytop Road, Suite 110
Syracuse, NY 13244–5290
Phone: 315–443–5534
Fax: 315–443–5545
supress@syr.edu
syracuseuniversitypress.syr.edu

Typesetting by Arlen House

All internal images and the back cover painting are by Denise
Jenkinson, and are reproduced courtesy of the artist's estate

The front cover painting of Prague is by Valeri

LOTTERY FUNDED

CONTENTS

ACKNOWLEDGEMENTS

Many thanks to the editors of journals where versions of these stories have appeared: 'Irish-Australian' was first published in *Southword* in 2020.

Thanks to Damian Smyth for driving me on as a writer, and to the Arts Council of Northern Ireland for funding these stories through their Artists Emergency Programme.

Thanks to Alan Hayes, and to John Baucher and Christine for helping me with my mother's paintings and, most importantly, thanks to all the larger-than-life characters who have let me share their experiences and their drink.

Thanks to Valeri for the painting of Prague.

Thanks to copyright holders for text from:
'I Don't Know How to Love Him' from *Jesus Christ Superstar*, written by Andrew Lloyd Webber (music) and Tim Rice (lyrics).
'There Are Worse Things I Could Do' from *Grease*, written by Warren Casey and Jim Jacobs.
'Don't Rain on My Parade' from *Funny Girl*, written by Jule Styne and Bob Merrill.
'Wannabe' written by the Spice Girls, Matt Rowe and Richard Stannard.
'The Crime of Castlereagh' by Bobby Sands.

Triste est omne animal post coitum, præter mulierem gallumque
All animals are sad after sex except for the woman and the rooster
Galen of Pergamum

MARCHING SEASON

THE A, B AND C'S OF MODERN LIVING

I'm not a fervent believer in nominative determinism, but there are some men whose names are deeply redolent of sex. For instance, Sam Rockwell is bound to be great in bed, and Robert Downey Jr was surely born to go down on women. And imagine how vigorous the poet, Ezra Pound, would have been.

I'd recently moved into a house with my friend, Leona, and we were having teething problems. In fact, it was more one giant toothache in the form of Gerard, her brand new boyfriend. He wasn't such a bad guy; he was an all-Ireland champion uilleann piper, and I could see why Leona liked him as he was dexterous with his fingers, but he had a hacking cannabis cough that reverberated through the house, and he kept mooching about in his boxer shorts all day, laughing at corny gifs on his phone, until it was time for the pub. Considering I was an artist, and also liked mooching about on my own, this arrangement was never going to work. It was crazy. I'd ended up living in a *ménage à trois* – without any of the benefits.

Luckily, I landed a studio space down the road for three months and was able to retreat there every day. The studio next door was occupied by a performance artist, Deirdre, who did naked dance moves in the mirror all afternoon and then draped herself in fabrics. When I told her the price of my paints, she urged me to ditch the painting and join her. She was off to do a performance protest in Guatemala, and offered to include me in her funding application. I might have been tempted to use my body as a blank canvas, but the problem was I didn't have her artistically imposing 36D breasts. Mine, while perfectly adequate for civilian duty, didn't have the gravitas required. Plus, and most importantly, I wanted to create art that would outlast my body, but naturally I didn't tell Deirdre that.

I was in the middle of painting a series of works provisionally titled 'Male Muses'. It would have been larger had I actually kept in touch with more of the guys I'd hooked up with, but it consisted of four exes who agreed to model for me. Because there were only four, I began to think about all the men I could have had sex with in my life. I was thirty seven now, but in my twenties I'd turned down quite a lot of men because:

(a) I was in a relationship
(b) I cockily considered myself too beautiful for them
(c) I enjoyed exercising my capricious elusive sex goddess power
(d) the alcohol was wearing off.

Looking back though, I couldn't help regret missing out on some beautiful men.

Maybe these feelings were intensified by living with Leona and Gerard; witnessing their little murmured kisses, tender strokes and blandishments. There was nothing like being around love for making you want to love.

A few days later, I went to the summer reception held by the Secretary of the Irish Department of Foreign Affairs.

Secretary in politics apparently meant 'chief' and not some admin person. A sure sign you were doing well in the art world was getting invited to such dos, and I didn't mind being a token artist as long as it got me some beer tokens.

It was one of those warm, grey summer evenings when my taxi turned off the Malone Road into a leafy lane. The actual house was pretty hideous, all reinforced concrete with dark, bulletproof windows, a relic from the Troubles. I shook the hand of the Secretary, scored a beer in a fancy glass and went through to the garden. The grass was beautifully manicured and overlooked by giant beech trees on the hillside.

The garden was also sprouting journalists, politicians, CEOs, twitterati, and community leaders, the latter including quite a few reformed paramilitaries. I spotted another artist being swooned over by a couple of women, but I didn't join him. I rarely got swooned over, which wasn't down to me so much as to the simple fact that men were less sapiosexual than women. Instead, I downed my beer, refilled it and threw myself into the mix.

I sidled over to a comedian I knew from TV who was standing on his own. He had a really bright red nose, so I guessed he liked a good drink. It was bulbous too like a clown's.

'All these journos and politicos,' I said. 'I wonder why we were invited?'

'Because we are people of influence.'

'Under the influence,' I laughed, tilting my glass.

He didn't even smile.

A woman came up and hugged him. I knew her face from Twitter, and she knew of me too.

'Talking of which,' she said, getting her phone out. 'Let's do a post.'

'Great,' I said, flicking my hair back. The gallery owners were always telling me to be more prominent on social media.

'You take it,' she said, handing me her phone.

Disgruntedly, I snapped her and the comedian cosying up, raising their glasses, then headed straight for another refill. Next, I wandered over to the smokers. The Green Party leader was smoking her head off and sucking on a beer bottle.

'Ah, straight from the bottle,' I said.

'Yeah, cuts out the washing-up. More ecological.'

'Right.'

'No, it's just because I'm a hallion,' she laughed.

I liked her.

A glossy business exec called me over to her table. 'Hey, Cora, tell everyone the story of you and me at Stormont.'

Story? My mind panicked. We'd been guest speakers in a line-up at Stormont, but there was no story. Fortunately, she couldn't bear to lose the limelight for one second and swept on with 'smokers are the coolest people, aren't they, Cora?'

'They so are,' I agreed. 'If you're not afraid to die, you're not afraid to live.'

She offered me a slim white cigarette from a flashy gold case, but frankly I was much too afraid to die.

I ambled off for another refill, chatting to an ex-rugby star on the way. The canapés were doing the rounds but I was too busy chatting to partake. Soon, I kept asking people their names again, getting names wrong, ending up with business cards I would lose later. After another beer I offered to join up a top diplomat's freckles with a pen. Around me, the dusk was blowing through the garden and the guests were thinning out. I finished my drink and phoned a taxi.

'Hey, Cora.' Someone was tapping me on the shoulder.

I turned to see a guy I didn't recognise.

'Remember, it's me, Connal?'

'Oh, god, yeah!'

Connal Power was a musician I hadn't seen in about eight years. I hardly knew him with his cropped silvery hair. He used to have long, curly blond hair framing his fine features. He was the sort of guy you might have called pretty but for his slatey eyes and muscles.

'I know,' he said, running his hand over his head. 'I'm fifty now. I'm a silver fox.'

'Well, I'm a red vixen,' I replied, and he laughed.

An image of him kept running through my mind from years before.

'Let's go out for a drink some time,' I said.

'Yeah, great.' He entered his number into my phone, all the time chatting about how he'd been away playing music in the USA and Australia.

I would have talked more but my taxi was waiting. I hurried out the sliding glass doors, narrowly avoiding decapitation from the hanging flower baskets wheeling around in the wind.

It was only when I got into the taxi with a stone-cold sober driver that I realized how drunk I was. My voice sounded slow, loud and slurred like a record on a low revolution. I didn't bother trying to make small talk but let the taxi take me back to my road with its tanning salons and dog-grooming salons or dog-tanning salons or whatever the trend was these days. I gave my pocket a squeeze just to check that my phone was still there. It was.

The next morning, Leona gave off to me about the cans in the recycling bag. I hadn't pushed the sharp lids down deep into the tins, and Gerard was angry about it as he'd nearly cut his finger.

'He needs his fingers for his pipes,' Leona added. 'It's his livelihood.'

What did he think I was going to do, dedigitate him? After all, I needed my fingers for my paintings too. What were his fingers made of, cotton wool? But I kept the peace and agreed to take more care next time. As I left the house for my studio, I could hear that barking cannabis cough from the upstairs window.

At the studio, Deirdre asked if she could use my left ear. She was planning to dance in Guatemala in a dress made of wax ears, at some protest to do with the Guatemalan government not hearing the pleas of people in poverty. I let her make a cast of my ear, feeling the plaster of Paris worm into the lining in my aural canal like a tongue. God, everything was turning me on in these hot, clammy summer days. I couldn't help thinking about my body. I didn't want to just make art with it, I wanted to live life with it.

The minute my ear was free, I composed a text to Connal Power: *Want to meet for a drink sometime soon? X*

I debated whether the kiss was too much, then thought, fuck it, it's not a work of art, just send it.

He texted back a few minutes later: *I usually go to the Sunflower Sat night if you fancy a drink?*

There was no kiss, so I guessed (a) he was playing it cool or (b) he only wanted to be friends. I texted back: *Gr8, see you 9.30 tomorrow.*

I kept seeing a vision of Connal sixteen years ago, one spring night. My friend Kate and I had met him and his friend Danny in the pub and gone back to Connal's house for a party. We drank, chatted, smoked weed till dawn. They got guitars out at one point and played a few tunes for us. I was attracted to Connal, but at about 5am he started ranting about something. I think it might have been about Protestants, and he maybe didn't know I was one.

Anyway, I didn't like his vitriol and, at that point, I made the decision to not sleep with him. At 6.30am the sun was blasting through the window and Danny was kissing Kate. I said I was going, and Connal followed me out and kissed me on the cheek in the hall.

'Do you not want to come to bed?' he asked, holding on tight to me.

I almost melted, but (a) I had work at 9.30 (b) my hangover was kicking in and (c) I had already decided. So I left.

Saturday was a hot, sunny day. I felt a hummingbird quiver in my stomach about meeting Connal Power but kept myself busy and picked Deirdre up for a drive round Belfast. She was on the lookout for suitable roofs or high walls where she might pose topless. I pointed out the Balls on the Falls as a good location.

'Yeah, perfect. I could always sit on top as a protest against penile oppression,' enthused Deirdre.

'Or scrotal oppression.'

We parked the car and ran through the traffic to what was basically a big steel globe with a mini-globe within, constructed on a roundabout. We started climbing up, to see if it was possible. Passing cars were tooting at us.

'Go all the way to the top, Cora,' Deirdre urged, but one of my feet slipped a little which gave me a fright. I clung on, imagining the headlines the next day:

CORA HARPER, LOCAL ARTIST, 37, DIES IN FALLS BALLS FALL

Cora Harper, the acclaimed local artist, died yesterday in a misadventure ascending the Rise sculpture in West Belfast. Her artist friend, Deirdre McKernan, internationally renowned for her nude performance art, tried to save her but to no avail. 'A great talent has left the art world,' said McKernan, who is planning an exciting trip to Guatemala.

Naturally, I'd prefer to be designated an international artist and not a local one, but I suddenly realised I needed to take action to ensure that. Shaky-legged, I headed back down. As soon as I stepped on to the earth, I told Deirdre that I was coming to Guatemala.

At home, I made myself a big life-affirming stir-fry. I never actually do cooking; it's just heating and eating. I put a lot of mushrooms in and they smelt so great Leona came into the kitchen.

'Where did you get those mushrooms?'

'The market. *Mmm.* Aren't they great?'

She checked the oil in the cupboard.

'Jesus fuck, I knew it,' she raged.

'What?'

'You've just tipped twenty quid's worth of my truffle oil into your pan!'

'No!' I kind of half-laughed which infuriated her even more. 'Sorry, Leona.'

I honestly hadn't noticed the label, but it explained the aroma. I told her I'd pay her back without much conviction and she stomped out. It seemed a trifle over a truffle, but I could hear her above the spitting oil giving off to Gerard in the living room about me. In this summer of open windows, there were no secrets. Things were reaching boiling point as well as frying point.

The Sunflower was one of the hippest bars in Belfast. It still retained the retro-grit of the security cage on its front door from the Troubles, while being colourful and quirky and covered in trippy street art. Connal wasn't at the packed bar, so I went through to the beer garden. The tables were full but I noticed he'd nabbed a standing spot near the pizza oven. He kissed me on the cheek when he saw me and introduced me to his friends who peeled away pretty quickly.

He looked so good in his black leather jacket, black t-shirt and jeans under the low lighting, but a strong smell of garlic suffused his breath. He asked me about my art and we both basked in the fact we were doing what we loved. He told me about his daughter of thirty two and how, just like him, she'd had a daughter at eighteen, but had recently put her daughter on the pill to break the cycle. He explained he'd never wanted to get married because his parents had violently argued before they'd split up, to the point where as a kid he used to sit in his bed at night and rock for hours.

'Do you want kids, Cora?' he asked.

'Yes and no. I think I'd rather be an artist.'

'If it's a decision between art and kids, it's going to put too much pressure on your art.'

He was right, but I didn't want to think about it.

I kept looking at his face. It was smooth and pale with barely a blemish, which was unusual for a man. Of course, there were a few wrinkles but he wore them well. He told me about his mother who lived in a care home and kept ringing him at maddening hours of the day. I could hear that anger from years before swelling in his voice, but I sympathised and he softened. He kept the chatter up, hardly allowing us room to breathe, but sometimes I could hear his voice rev on the same word in some ghost of a stammer. I understood he wasn't nervous around me, it was just that kids who stammer grow up into adults who talk too fast.

He took out his vaper and sucked on it.

'Whoah. Is that grass?'

'Yeah, but it's healthy this way. It steams the marijuana rather than burning it.'

'You make it sound like you're lightly steaming some broccoli there!'

'Well, it's still pretty healthy. I also eat chopped garlic in a spoonful of honey every morning.'

'I can tell.'

'Really?'

'It's grand,' I said and I was aware I didn't even smell it anymore. I was now under his spell, under his scent.

A skiff of rain arrived. We thought about moving under the big white canopy which looked tie-dyed with green algae, but it felt freeing to be under the sky. Connal took out his phone and mapped the stars with a constellation app.

'Show me Mars,' I asked, and he located it. It was hanging low like it was sitting in the aperture of the pizza oven. All I could think of was a big red tomatoey pizza.

We went to the bar for another pint of Kozel. I noticed his t-shirt had the name of a band, 'Poisoned Girls', emblazoned across his chest.

'Should I check this pint?' I asked, feigning worry.

'Why?'

'Do you go round poisoning girls much?'

'Yeah. All the time,' he laughed.

'That's cool. I murder boys too.'

I felt dazed and chilled from the warm night and the drink. Some young artists said hi as they passed.

'Fancy one more in the Spaniard?' Connal asked.

A lightning image of those blond curls flashed through my mind.

'I thought maybe you'd like to come back to mine.'

He looked perplexed. 'But I thought we'd always just been mates.'

'It's ok if you don't want to,' I heard myself say as the past slipped away. Right now it felt almost as far away as Mars. 'But I'd really like to.'

I could almost see the image of it passing his eyes.

'Yeah then ... If you come to my place instead.'

'I'd love to.'

It was getting late so we drank up and I left the dregs of my pint. He was all business, ringing the taxi, suggesting walking round to the Kremlin where we could get a taxi even quicker. I could tell he was excited, as he was urgent, energetic. When we got into the taxi, his legs were sprawled out, so one was touching mine, and his arm was on top of mine, holding my hand.

We got out at his Victorian, three-storeyed red-brick at the top of the Limestone Road. From the outside it didn't look familiar. I remembered he'd rented rooms out to pay his mortgage sixteen years ago, and he told me he was still renting them out. The hall we went into was huge but bare. It felt like an institution. He unlocked his private living room on the ground floor. It all flooded back to me, being here, the huge windows, the high ceiling, but it felt blue then, and the walls now were warm terracotta red and cream. I was wondering if memories of missed moments were blue-tinged round the edges.

We went into the kitchen.

'I only have one beer left. I'll have to order some in.'

'No worries. We'll share it.'

He poured the beer into a couple of large crystal wine glasses.

'Just to put on the style,' he grinned.

When I sipped from the glass, there was a chip in it.

We went back through to the living room. He told me all about the artefacts on the walls; the Moroccan masks he'd haggled over, the guitars hanging up, some of which were worth a fortune, and the prints of Vermeer, Klimt and Monet. He talked nonstop as if to cover up that the only thing of value to us there tonight was each other's body.

'The Monet is meant to be a sunrise but I think it looks like a sunset.'

'I think it looks like a sunset too,' I said and a feeling came over me of having no sense of time. He lit some huge white candles on the old marble mantelpiece. The flames flickered deep below the thin wax cliffs.

'You don't mind if I do a line of coke, do you?' he checked, flipping a small bag onto the coffee table.

I wasn't sure he was offering, but I told him anyway that I don't do coke, not since a couple of really bad sinus infections. The first infection I had, my nose streamed so much I developed a scab on it, and went to my own exhibition launch looking like a disreputable street junkie.

'It was probably thirty quid a gram crap. This coke costs a hundred a g.'

As soon as he snorted, he turned and kissed me. He was a good kisser and I could feel him licking my teeth. He put his hand on mine and steered it onto the bulge in his jeans, while his fingers pushed down the gap at the back of my jeans. His other hand grabbed my left breast and roughly dug into my flesh.

'Take your clothes off,' he said, and we both quickly peeled them off. The one thing I noticed was that his chest was hairless and his pubes were almost non-existent. He was as well groomed as a model; in fact, he reminded me of a Renaissance painting.

'Wow. No hair,' I said.

'Maybe I over-trimmed.'

His cock was a good size and I sucked it. It tasted fresh, seasoned with a little saltiness. He sighed while his fingers reached inside me. He seemed sensitive but he had no finesse. He pulled me on top of him. There wasn't much room on this sofa for complex positions. He dived in quick and his cock hit hard against my aridity. It hurt as he kept forcing it like an insistent locksmith and a cry crept out of my mouth, so he moved me onto my back. My flesh began to resist as his belly started slap-slap-slapping against mine, making the sound of a sweat-drenched boxing glove on skin. Whenever he pulled back to put more force into it, he slipped out and I had to guide him back in.

He lived up to his name; he did have power. It struck me that Connal talked fast because of his childhood stammer, and he liked to have sex that way too. Funnily enough, he reminded me of a stallion I was once on that only had two speeds – trot and gallop. The stallion didn't know how to canter, and burst into such a gallop I nearly broke my neck on a branch. Breakneck sex, I kept thinking to myself.

I felt that I had an insight into Connal's being, his soul, his DNA. My female friends often said of the men they slept with, 'he's just a shag,' but the truth was no man was 'just' a shag and they were all so different, and if Eve tasted the apple in the Garden of Eden I wanted to taste every type of apple in that garden too: ambrosia, winesap, redlove, cox's pippin, russet, braeburn, bramley, angel bites, strawberry cheeks, bloody butchers, Irish peaches, foxes whelps ...

He continued to go in and out fast, bucking like a bronco that couldn't get a phantom rider off his back, foaming inside me with pumped-up purple rage, leaving me raw and swollen. We must have been shaking the wall hard, as a guitar fell down on top of us – the one that cost four thousand pounds – and he pulled out, leapt off me and laid it reverentially on the ground. Clearly you had to be made of wood to be treated softly. I sucked him for a while as he bunched the back of my hair with his fingers to the same rhythm. Again he steered my hand over to his balls and moved my legs apart with the dexterity of a puppet master. This time, the fire had gone out and we returned thirstily to our last sips of beer.

'Do you use Viagra?'

'I have done,' he shrugged. 'But not tonight.'

'I thought most guys over fifty used it these days.'

'I've never had any problems that way.'

'Right.'

'Must be the garlic and honey. And the olive oil I cook with.'

'Ha, I've heard that truffle oil is good too,' I said, thinking ruefully of Leona and Gerard.

I checked my watch and saw it was nearly 3am. An hour and a half had passed on that couch. It didn't seem possible we'd been fused together for so long.

'Time I left.'

'Let me play you something first.'

'I guess that guitar was begging to be played, whacking us on the head there.'

'No kidding. I'll play you Nick Drake.'

'I know the name.'

'He died young.'

He played me a couple of songs, still naked, and I watched his muscles running through his forearm, and the emotion on his face. The music was the part I remembered from before. We put our clothes on and he phoned for a taxi.

When I was out in the hall, I recalled how years ago he'd asked me to stay, how he'd held on to my arm, even as I said I was going, and how I'd looked back at him, full of longing and rejection. It struck me that there were no a, b's, c's and d's in life, only a's; no reasons not to, only reasons to, and you had to act fast or lose everything.

I ran down the steps to the taxi, turned and blew him a gentle kiss. From the big bright hall, he blew me a kiss in return. I jumped in the taxi and it rolled away as I said goodbye for good.

MARCHING SEASON

Marcus was standing on Bangor pier watching the fishermen. He could hear the clink of the mooring hooks in the wind. One of the fishermen, his oilskins torn at the crotch, smiled at him, showing teeth like boulders, the veins roping through his arms like fishing lines as he lifted a heavy crate out of the hold, his biceps bearing the blurred tidemark between pale and weathered skin. Just as the fisherman turned away, the boom went swinging into his head, boom, boom, BOOM. In that instant of bizarre violence, Marcus realised he was in a dream, and swum up slowly from its wavering images.

He was sweating, semi-naked under his duvet, the sound of a Lambeg drum shaking the window in its frame. He hopped out of bed and peeped through the blinds. It was the kids again. Every frigging afternoon it was now. That wee seven-year-old boy with a mini-Lambeg strapped to his back, strong as a bull calf, while the other kids marched along, playing whistles, recorders, toy drums and crashing cymbals. Their band leader was an angry, bossy martinet of a thirteen-year-old girl, a Madison or a Chelsea if ever there was one. They were practising feverishly for the Twelfth of July, making sure they paraded down Castlereagh Street for the benefit of the Catholics in the Short Strand.

Marcus padded through to the bathroom, yawning, and washed his face with water. He looked tired, though his tan helped conceal it. His skin was so fine it was marked by the crease in the pillow. It almost matched the scar on his brow from the time that young hood had hit him.

13:37, his mobile informed him. He'd arrived home from his Dublin gig at six that morning, so it tallied up to just seven hours sleep. There was no point in going back to bed either as the Lambeg-lambaster was sure to do a circuit and return within the hour.

He put on his chinos with the Gucci belt and a white shirt, topping it off with a grey waistcoat that held his stomach in as tight as a corset. Not that he needed it as he was always slim in the summer.

His mobile rang. It was Conor, wanting to know how the show had gone in Dublin.

'Fab,' Marcus said, 'but I'm wrecked. The kids just woke me up. Junior Blood and Thunder.'

'See?' said Conor, sounding irked. 'I told you to come and move in with me. You mustn't be there for the Twelfth.'

'Oh, but it's all fine,' said Marcus, trying to smooth everything over. Conor was a West Belfast Catholic and didn't like visiting the loyalist east, even though Marcus lied and insisted it was cool, so long as you didn't camp it up too much. It was sweet Conor inviting him to move in, but they'd only been going out two months and, besides, there was no room at Conor's for all his things.

'Look, it's grand here as long as you keep your head down,' Marcus insisted. 'And I love to keep my head down on you, gorgeous,' he added, making Conor laugh.

They'd met on a night out at the Kremlin. Conor was there with a group of hetties, while Marcus was doing a brief set as Regina Grande and had sensed Conor's eyes on his body. Conor looked like the poet he was with his white shirt and long hanging cuffs, topped off with a baseball cap – an odd hybrid of beats and Keats, urban yet romantic. He sent conflicting signals to Marcus because he was vaguely femme in feature yet masculine in gesture. From his seat in the alcove, he crossed his leg in a masculine way, ankle across the knee.

After the show he'd come up to tell Regina how wonderful she was, then shyly turned away.

'Who's that little chicken?' asked another drag queen.

'I don't know,' Marcus said.

Marcus impulsively went over to Conor. He didn't know why because all his life he was the queen bee who waited to be attended on, circled by worker drones bringing honeyed compliments, but he somehow intuited that Conor was too different to let go.

'Where are you from?'

'Poleglass,' said Conor.

'Where's that near? The Virgin Islands?' Marcus joked, still in full Regina innuendo mode, but the more they talked, the more he cooled down on the shtick. He found out that Conor was bisexual, although his experiences with men sounded more like skirmishes than anything full-on.

'What *is* that?' Marcus asked of a small slab of what seemed to be ivory hanging round Conor's neck.

'It's bone. Scratch it with your nail and see.'

'Took me an age to do these,' said Marcus, showing his glittery fake nails, but he moved his fingers towards Conor's throat, feeling a tremor.

The surface of the soft bone came off on the tip of his nail, leaving a fresh white trail.

'Wow. It's not from the hip of your last lover, is it?'

'No, no,' laughed Conor. 'It's whale bone. I bought it in Morocco.'

At the end of the night, as everyone left, Trixie Dix said to Marcus, 'he's a cutie. You better keep an eye on him.'

Marcus licked his finger, drawing it down Conor's face and onto his neck. When he saw Conor's shocked expression, he regretted it, but Regina could be a bit OTT sometimes.

'He's all mine,' Marcus said, for Trixie's benefit, and he'd never been so sure of anything in his life.

Marcus headed out to the shop. It was the tenth of July, the day before bonfire night, and there was a distinct smell of burning in the air, signifying that arsonists had got to a bonfire ahead of time. A few rosettes of smoke were frilling the blue sky and a tiny dot of a helicopter danced through the plumes. He couldn't help noticing that the passersby were all rushing towards the smoke, further into the east. It was strange how the kerbs were sprouting yellow grass, as if in the bright sunshine they were bursting into flames.

He shrugged and walked on. He was thinking of the show he was MCing that night in the Sunflower. It was called Viva la Diva and there was burlesque, a circus act, a dance act ... He quickly ran through his inventory of risqué jokes. What do you call a group of male dancers who all go on the piss? A dance droop. It wasn't great, but with the right delivery ... He was also planning his grand entrance, singing Rizzo's song in *Grease*. His voice gave him the edge over most of the other queens who lip-synched.

In the local shop, the radio was on and the tills fell silent as everyone listened in:

A second bonfire is currently being removed in east Belfast under police guard. Contractors wearing masks to protect their identity are dismantling the bonfire in Cluan Place. The police have just issued a statement that the pyre is posing 'a significant risk to people and property in the area ...'

'Unsafe my arse,' interrupted a customer. 'That bonefire has been there for years. Four weeks to build and the bastards pull it down in four hours.'

'Destroying our culture,' said one of the workers, Leanne, popping her head over the crisp section where she was busy restocking. 'Giving the Protestant people a hard time, eh, Marcus?'

Marcus made a faint murmur of sympathy to show he was in support, then went up to the till with milk, wheaten bread and sweets. He picked up an Aero on the way that said *'For Sharing'*. Share? I'll have that scarfed in two seconds, Marcus laughed to himself. It was strange how Conor had no taste for the sweet and loved savoury. A sensation ran through his head of Conor's tangy body.

Outside, another helicopter was heading eastwards like a flashing firefly. The air rocked with the sound of a blast bomb, making Marcus's chest jolt. It was far enough away not to worry him, but there was bound to be trouble on the streets tonight. Christ, it was hard to get taxis at the best of times on a Friday, but with mad-ass loyalists losing the run of themselves there would be little chance. Taxis wouldn't risk a brick through the windscreen, or even worse getting hijacked and burnt out.

'I'll leave the flat early,' Marcus decided. Cool it, he told himself, feeling the sun on his face. It was so bright he even had to squint through his sunglasses.

Turning into his street, the overgrown bush on the corner thrust out its roses as though presenting him with a bouquet. He couldn't help feeling he'd give a great show that night. He was almost home when his neighbour, Robert, stepped out, beckoning him into his flat.

'Marcus, Marcus,' he was calling croakily from his quivering chins. He was a pitiful sight with his greying whiskers and yellow-tinged eyes.

'Hi Robert. Everything ok?' Marcus said, coming through Robert's door.

'Could you put these numbers in?' Robert asked. 'My hands are gone.'

The receipt was shaking like a petal in his fingers. The DTs again, thought Marcus, going into the bottle-strewn living room, bending over and punching the numbers into the electric meter. The dogs were leaping up onto his back, frantic from being locked in all day.

'How's the form with you? Any shows on the go?' Robert was asking. Ever since Marcus had moved in, he'd been fascinated by Regina.

'Yep, a big show on tonight, Robert.'

'There'll be a big show here too,' winked Robert.

'I know. I heard there's trouble.'

Robert was university-educated but the drinking had dragged him down to this ground floor flat. It smelt of dog's urine and cigarette smoke, and the wallpaper was peeling into scrolls. The layer of dust and fag ash on everything was as bad as Pompeii. The skirting boards were covered in dog hair like they were trying to self-insulate from the coldness of the walls. There was a rumour going round that Robert hid guns here for the UDA.

'I'd better go,' said Marcus.

'Aye, I imagine it takes some time, all that exfoliating and that,' said Robert.

'More plucked than a turkey, me,' laughed Marcus, hurrying out.

He headed up to his own flat, taking a moment to luxuriate in its cleanliness. He noticed the tall thin cactus in the pot by the wall and recalled how Conor had pointed it out the morning after their first night together. The implication was that Marcus didn't have a nurturing soul and couldn't be bothered to look after anyone but himself.

A little wooden bird was hanging from one of the cactus spikes. No more than a cutout reflecting his own make-believe, fake world, mused Marcus. It was funny how being viewed through someone else's eyes made you question yourself.

He went into the bathroom and started lathering the acrid-smelling Immac onto his legs. He'd done his legs two days ago but even the faintest of hair growth bothered him. There had been that one time in bed years ago when a Czech man had raised his face from Marcus's balls and stuck his tongue out in displeasure as if he'd licked sandpaper. It was true that the memory of one single flinch could scar you.

He started to sing. Maybe he'd strut on instead to 'I'm Gorgeous' from *The Apple Tree*. Maybe he'd start the second half with 'I Don't Know How to Love Him' from *Jesus Christ Superstar* – now that would get them eating out of his hand. As a kid he used to love sitting with his sister watching the old musicals while his brother killed soldiers on some computer game. That was when he knew beyond doubt that he was different, some crossbreed, some boy-girl fusion. He'd been so glad to leave his family home in the village, the gospels written in giant letters on the gable end of barns, the stifling whin, broom and vetch of the country roads. The only time his father had ever mentioned his 'act', he'd paused heavily before uttering the word.

At eight years old at school in Bangor, he'd had his first crush on a boy. Tyler Girvan. Tyler Girvan had blond hair and wore a leather jacket. After lunch, when the teacher shouted for them to get in line, Marcus would race across the playground just so he could stand behind Tyler Girvan and breathe in his leather musk, the sweet scent of his blond hair. As blond as Conor. It seemed that his earliest sexual fantasy had infused his whole life.

I don't know how to love him
what to do, how to move him
I've been changed, yes really changed
in these past few days
when I've seen myself
I seem like someone else.

With every word he kept thinking of Conor.

He opened his Aero in the bath, ate a few cubes and felt decadent – bubbles in bubbles. A glass of Prosecco and he'd be well sorted. His skin felt so soft and feminine in the water. He would have felt ultra-relaxed but for the clash of cutlery from the open kitchen windows. It was teatime, but he was always too keyed up before a show to eat more than a sweet or two.

He finally got out of the bath, dried himself and put on his bra and thong. It was an industrial strength thong to keep his bits in place. He remembered the time Conor had put on his red spangly dress for fun and how he'd bulged through it.

'God, I need to be strapped down,' Conor had grinned.

'I'll strap you down any day, Con,' Marcus had said, kissing him.

Shouts from the street cut through his thoughts. He slung on his dressing gown and hurried down to the front door. A gang of about a dozen teens was heading towards the bonfire, all on the balls of their toes, weaving with the anger of wasps. Some wore hoodies and scarves, others balaclavas, resembling black insect heads. One of the teens was looking straight at him through the slits of the balaclava and made a chopping motion at his throat just as Marcus drew back and slammed the door shut. Marcus immediately berated himself for not staying inside; he should never have shown his face. Teens here were paranoid about neighbours touting on them. Sure on nearly every street corner there were slogans about so-and-so being a tout.

He told his beating heart not to be so scared. He was just up to high doh about the show, that was all. But it was mad how he'd always had a nose for strolling into trouble. That night a few years ago when, as Regina, he'd got out of the taxi on his road only to get a punch in the side of the temple that burst his skin.

The punch was the real reason he didn't want to move in with Conor, why he insisted on staying in his flat over the Twelfth. He didn't want to admit to his fear and, if he moved out, the boy who punched him would win, but by staying he could change things. Sure they all accepted him now in the shop, the likes of Robert loved him. If he left, it would throw up the old memories of how he had to leave home, how he had had to suppress his true self for years. If only he could talk to Conor, but Conor's hatred of the Twelfth was inbred, and he would never understand Marcus's desire to reconcile himself with the culture around him. It sounded mad but there was something that had always thrilled Marcus about the rhythm and colour of parades, the swagger and strut of the drum major, twirling his baton like a dancer from a musical with a cane ...

He slipped the falsies into his bra. Born again breasts, he liked to call them. He sat down at his makeup table and opened the huge slabs of concealer, powder, liners, lippies, brushes bigger than you'd paint your house with ... Each layer he applied was as thick as an epidermis, transforming him completely.

He'd been born from a caesarian. He came from a cut. It always struck him that he'd scarred his mother from the get-go. Sometimes he'd joke he'd never even been out of a vagina, let alone inside one. Up to the age of four, he was coldrife and he'd sneak into his mum's bed for warmth while his father was off doing night shift. One night, when he was lying on top of his mother's body, she told him to stop rubbing himself. Her words had become lodged in his mind and, at times, he wondered if it was her disapproval that had put him off women forever.

He put on his dress, smoothed his body into it, the heat of his hands almost ironing the fabric. Then put on his honey-brown wig. In the mirror, she looked wonderful, chimeric. Up above, he could hear the whirr of rotor blades. Ah, my private helicopter's arrived, he smiled, but he guessed it heralded trouble. He quickly booked a taxi. It was nine thirty and the evening had run away with itself. The last of the slanting sunlight was squeezing itself between the tight seams of the buildings.

As soon as the taxi arrived, he looked out through the window to check the street was clear. He pulled on his raincoat to cover up his dress and ran out. Each time he left the house as Regina he double-checked there were no groups of young men walking past. His neighbours were cool but he still had to take care.

The taxi sped away, the eyes of the driver wide as he sussed out Marcus in his rearview mirror. The sky was glazed with a soft rosy nacre as the night pushed down the pearl of the sun onto the horizon.

'There'll be murder on tonight,' said the taxi driver darkly.

'The next act, ladies, ladyboys and gentlemen, is a brand new and exceedingly muscular group. They're all brawn and no brain. Did I say prawn? No, I know prawn's no good, hon, I meant brawn. So please give it up for the amazing and fantabulous Flawless!'

As he stepped back into the wings, the dance act running past him, he thought he could see Conor come in through the low lighting, half crouching to find himself a seat. He looked again just to make sure; it was definitely him. It was the first night since they'd met that Conor had come to one of his shows.

Once the act was over, Marcus threw himself into his valedictory number. He sang it to Conor, praying that they'd make it, that they'd stay together.

I could hurt someone like me
out of spite or jealousy
I don't steal
and I don't lie but I can feel
and I can cry
a fact I'll bet you never knew
but to cry in front of you
that's the worst thing I could do-oo.

'Oh my god, I can't believe you're here!' Marcus cried out, bouncing over to Conor once the applause had died away.

'I heard about the riots. I thought I'd better take you home with me.'

Trixie Dix loomed into vision, planting a huge kiss on Marcus's cheek.

'Honey, you were amazing,' Trixie Dix enthused. She glanced down at the bouquet in Marcus's arms and quipped, 'what's better than flowers on the grand piano? Tulips on your organ. Gettit? Two lips!'

'If shit was wit you'd be Oscar Wilde,' one of the other queens sneered.

Marcus was caught up in a festoon of congratulations. At one point he glanced over at Conor to see him chatting to some girls. It gave him a jealous pang, knowing Conor was bisexual. But yet he, Marcus/Regina, was bi-imaged, one part man, one part woman, so surely he was more than enough for him.

'Keep your eye on that one,' came Trixie's bitchy whisper. 'A good shepherdess always looks after her cock, I mean flock.'

'Oh, don't worry, he's looking after me. Making sure I don't get caught up in the riots.'

'Here, Conor, you better look after Regina tonight. She goes wild for helicopters. Everyone knows she loves a big chopper.'

'Trixie, your routine is as stale as your breath, honey,' one of the queens sighed.

'C'mon, lover,' said Marcus, interlocking arms with Conor. 'Let's go to yours.'

He tripped out of the Sunflower on a high. He was vaguely aware he towered above Conor in his heels, but what did it matter?

In Conor's car, Marcus kept envisioning the teenage boy in the balaclava like a bad dream.

'Conor, do you mind if we pop home to mine first?'

'But it's dangerous.'

'My street isn't next to the bonfire. Don't fret, honey. I'll direct you. I just need to check that no one's put a brick through the window.'

He wanted to tell Conor about the boy giving him the throat sign, but was scared to give voice to his own paranoia. As they drove down past the Big Fish, they could see the flashes of helicopters circling above the east.

They turned into the Woodstock Road and carried on up towards the Mount. The mephitic fumes of arson tainted the air. Cars were parking on the roadside, disgorging young loyalists chattering excitedly, carryouts in hand as if they were heading to a street festival. The moon hung low and large and orange from the glow of the city lights.

As Conor drove into Marcus's street, he slammed on the brakes. Fifty metres away was a crowd facing a line of riot police decked out in their baggie blues. It was a Mexican standoff, both parties waiting for the other to attack.

'Fuck, fuck, fuck,' panicked Conor, trying to reverse, crunching the gears.

'Wait, Conor, stop,' said Marcus. 'Let me out here.'

Marcus shoved open the door. Amidst the shudder of the copter blades, random shouts rang out from the crowd. An emergency vehicle wailed.

Marcus hurried towards his flat and saw, to his relief, there was no damage to the windows. Straight ahead, he could hear music blaring from the riot; behind him, Conor had managed to park the car. Laughter peeled out above the music. On an impulse, he walked on.

'Marcus!' Conor called after him, but he didn't turn. He stumbled over some bricks, rocks and bottles littering the road. He cursed as a brick scuffed his heel. Weaving his way through the crowd, he could see a drunken guy doing some sort of impromptu breakdance in the middle of the road, birling round on his scoliotic back like a fat-limbed tortoise, while everyone clapped and egged him on. As someone switched off the music, the man staggered off dizzily. Regina, sensing the opening, stepped forward into the empty semicircle. The staccato clip of her own heels thrilled her. The lights of the police land rovers and the water cannon were trained on her.

> Don't tell me not to live
> just sit and putter
> life's candy and the sun's
> a ball of butter
> don't bring around a cloud
> to rain on my parade.

He could hear the gasps around him. 'What the fuck?' growled a deep voice behind him. There was ugliness, sourness in the air, but he ignored it and carried on singing. He didn't care anymore. Let them beat him to death if they wanted. He was going to be who he was in this community. Some titters began to take hold.

He felt a hand grabbing his bum, but he spun out of the way without breaking beat with the song. Someone threw a punch at him, but it skimmed him and he sang on, sensing his aggressor being dragged back into the crowd.

He could see Robert, drink in hand, lumber over, shouting, 'go on there, girl. Give it some rice!' Leanne was looking on bright-eyed from the shadows.

A drunk girl in a short skirt was dancing next to him, showing her bum to the crowd.

'Yeoh!' the men shouted.

I'm not afraid, I'm not afraid, I'm not afraid, went the backing group within Marcus's head. His voice soared. The spotlights of the vehicles went on full beam. He could hear the riot police flip back their visors, drawn in, spellbound.

Get ready for me, love
cause I'm a commer
I simply gotta march
my heart's a drummer
nobody, no, nobody
is gonna rain on my parade.

LIFE IS SHORT AND FUN SHOULD BE HAD

Hey Cora ...

I'd just started a new job, had moved into a rented house on my own and was getting over a bad breakup with a man. Or should that have been a breakup with a bad man? Luke was his name and he'd been caught some years ago for possession of speed and coke. My parents, frightened of what the rellies might think of his criminal past, had said at the start, 'whatever you do, don't let it get out.' They made going out with him sound like having coronavirus.

I was happy to be distracted by my new job and concentrate my energies on fiddling flexitime rather than mourning Luke. I worked in the scanning department, feeding the documents of disability claimants into a giant scanner that roared louder than an aircraft on takeoff. I was just relieved I wasn't on data input, as I was achingly slow on computers. To be honest, I'd always preferred to run my fingers up and down bodies than keyboards.

Which was why, with the encouragement of a work colleague, I'd put my profile on Tinder. The moment I gave in, I regretted it. I wasn't ready in the same way I wasn't ready to go back to painting. I'd used my artist's grant on nights out drinking with Luke and had no cash left for materials. All I had left was a portrait of Luke in the spare room which was tied up in a plastic bag for fear of it reminding me of *The Picture of Dorian Gray*. All I could imagine was his face curled in contempt at my tragicomic single life.

However, when a man I knew called Leo facebooked me three months later, I jumped at the chance to meet up. I'd met him six years ago when we'd worked in adjoining offices at the Child Maintenance Service. Although I couldn't remember him that well I had a distinct image of him standing on the stairs, lips laced with a smouldering smile.

> *Hey Cora, how are things? I stumbled on you on Tinder the other day and I wasn't expecting that at all.*
>
> *That's hilarious, Leo. I put my profile up, but haven't even checked it yet. You getting many dates on it?*
>
> *No, but I hit like on you.*
>
> *I wouldn't even have known as I'm never on, but thanks for that!*
>
> *You should go on it. We might match (smiley face)*
>
> *Well if you want a date you can always ask on fb.*
>
> *Would you like to go out sometime, Cora? X*
>
> *That was quick! Yes, I would. Who needs Tinder?*
>
> *True, you could always put the kettle on and we could chill and catch up. X*

Within a minute, we'd agreed on a date and time. He texted back.

> *Where do you live? X*

I balked a second at the reality of it, as I hated giving out my phone number or address.

> *You're not a stalker, are you?*
>
> *What? Lol.*
>
> *I know. I'm a bit paranoid.*
>
> *No, I am not. Think you know that after we worked together. X*

'Working together' was pushing it as I'd barely known him. I sent my address, but something still bothered me. It was the speed and smoothness of the arrangement, the pushiness of him suggesting my house. Maybe it was just the way with cyberdating, but I went straight on to Google.

Leo's photo came up with ARRESTED across it in huge red letters. I clicked on the link below it, but it said there was no secure connection. I scrolled down to another link that said 'UK and Éireann Hunters' and clicked again:

> *Joint sting — Leo Monroe — Belfast — arrested grooming what he believed was a 12-year-old girl. Highly sexually explicit language.*

My stomach and chest flipped. The horror spread up to my face in a hot rush. I leapt back on to Messenger.

> *Sorry, Leo, I'd like to cancel that meeting. I've changed my mind completely. I'm not up for any relationships. Hope you don't mind and sorry for messing you around.*
>
> *Something I have done or something you have just found out?*
>
> *There's a picture of you on the internet about grooming. That's fairly off-putting.*

He sent me a long message back to say it was an old photo taken from his work profile, and that his identity had been stolen off his inactive Twitter account by a paedophile ring who later released his image to a paedo hunter blog to take the heat off themselves. The police had arrested him but four months later they gave him back his laptop and phone, the case against him dropped. When he'd asked Google to delete the post, they'd refused, insisting it was 'in the public interest'. He was now waiting for the Cyber Crime Unit to help him. It had been a terrible time as, due to being plastered all over the internet, he'd been sacked from the Child Maintenance Service.

> *Believe me, Cora, I am not a stalker or a child abuser in any way, shape or form. But I understand if you don't want to know me.*

Do I believe him, I wondered? It all sounded perfectly plausible, and I believed I believed him but there was always that aspect of not knowing the truth of someone. Unless you looked them in the eyes, you never really could tell if someone was lying or not. There's a phrase in Irish – 'the cat always reveals itself by its eyes'. Whatever the case, the reverberations from that photo were still shaking me.

I went to the office all through those winter months. I was that bored I took up smoking so I could earn two smoke breaks a day out in the courtyard. It was a welcome respite from the office – of course, I was guaranteed to knock a few years off my life with the smoke but, sure, why worry about the future. Outside work, I went on a few nights out, but didn't meet anyone. It was possible Luke had made me lose my confidence. The one time I'd broached having children together, he'd said to me 'but how would we get by? It's not like you have a good job or anything.' Clearly to him, love was secondary to having a healthy financial status.

I was thirty seven now, and on the positive side I'd travelled a great deal and met some amazing men, but all that really added up to was too many miles on the clock (take out the l). I felt in a sort of stasis. One night, sitting alone in the house, I looked up Leo's Facebook messages again. When I reread them, I felt the truth in his words and it struck me that I was potentially missing out on a great guy. Give him a chance, a voice kept telling me. Who are you to judge? The internet was a roiling mass of fakes and trolls and scammers who could bring down any innocent. Maybe I felt the vigour of spring in my bones, the buds breaking out in their brightly-coloured flesh and I longed to do something impulsive. Outside, the road was polka-dotted in white cherry blossom. There was a delicious stir in my fingertips, a restlessness I had to give in to. As Gwendolen said in *The Importance of Being Earnest*, 'I have the gravest doubts upon the subject. But I intend to crush them.'

A few days later, I spotted a curl of sandy brown on my pillow and my heart nearly split from its tethers – it was just like Luke's hair. When I looked closer it was only a tiny duck feather. I knew I was still haunted and I'd have to take a risk to move on. I went on Messenger once more, thinking to myself, keep it casual.

> *Leo, I'd still like to see you if you want to come around some afternoon for a cup of tea. Cheers, Cora.*

I kept looking back at the screen nervously. Finally, the ellipsis danced across the screen.

> *What changed your mind?*
> *Life is short and fun should be had! Are you free tomorrow?*

We arranged the meeting for the following afternoon. After a while, he came back.

> *Life is short and fun should be had!?*

He was asking me to be more explicit but I wanted to leave things vague, though I was pretty sure 'fun' or 'doing stuff' was the euphemism for sex online. I didn't know what to say because I didn't want to be crude or crass or break the whole magic of not knowing what might happen. It was frustrating for the romantic within me, especially when I knew ten seconds face to face could accomplish more than twenty messages. After a couple of false starts and deletions, I replied.

> *I don't know if we're on the right wavelength, but I meant chat, see if there's chemistry, then have fun if it works out that way.*
> *That's cool with me. We are on the same wavelength. X*

I had a quick gander round the house. It had already been in a bad state when I'd arrived. It was one of those tiny parlour houses a shipyard worker used to inhabit, the old outdoor toilet now housing a dilapidated boiler that roared and produced enough fumes to de-ecologise the whole district. The bathroom tiles were spotted with a coral pink damp which you could perhaps have described as a jaunty shade if you were putting a gloss on it, and believe me, the whole house needed a lick of gloss. The damp, I hasten to add, wasn't my fault as it was down to the ancient bath having a dip in its base which hosted a permanent pool of festering water. Rain had even got into the double glazing giving all the windows a misted-up, frosted effect. It was like living in a massive refrigeration unit, and the blue walls of my bedroom emitted an eerie suboceanic vibe, but at least the rent was affordable.

After a cursory spruce-up, I skipped round to the local Mace to buy some biscuits. Half the shelves were empty as if under some Soviet-style enforced rationing. In the absence of any luxury biscuiterie, I bought some Club Mint which I guessed he'd like since his taste was impeccable enough to like me.

It was dark; the glittering snail trails lighting up the pavements. At one point I could almost imagine a heart shape drawn with a silver glitter pen. That night I was so excited I couldn't sleep. Still, I was selfish, I had no solidarity with other women or abused children. What if I was rewarding a child abuser? But, these days, men weren't exactly beating down my bedroom door. A new guy would surely inspire me in my art, kick-start me in my creativity, renew my confidence. Besides, artists were beyond morality. Look at Francis Bacon who made a fortune out of painting his young, violently criminal lover. If it was alright for Francie, it was alright for me.

I kept trying to lower my body into the bed, imagining it sinking into the soft dream of the mattress, trying to stifle my solipsistic ramblings, but the thought of Leo was luring me along as though I was running through the dark streets chasing some *ignis fatuus*. I kept hearing a strange buzzing, as if my eardrum had been struck by a tuning fork. When I finally fell asleep I dreamt I was in hospital and a surgeon was about to operate on my heart. I woke up in a panic, my pulse racing, terrified the anaesthetic would kill me. All I could think of was my heart as a gourd leaking blood, and all I knew was I hadn't drunk fully from life.

Work the next day dragged. I had a dental appointment during my lunch break and got a new filling near the front. I was aghast when I got back to the office loos and saw that half my lip had subsided from the injection – I looked like a stroke victim! I left work at three thirty and hurried home. I quickly showered, then went up to the mirror in the landing to finger-brush my hair. It looked good – rich vulpine red in the late afternoon light. The aftereffects of the dentist still bothered me – my mouth seemed to taste of antibiotic and Savlon; he must have given me as much Novocaine as you'd give a horse because one side of my mouth hardly moved, meaning the other side sported an Elvis-style sneer when I smiled. It would be alright though, I reassured myself, as long as I didn't smile too much. I decided to go for the natural look with a fairy-dust sprinkling of makeup since I was in my own home and, besides, I didn't have much time.

Through my open bedroom window, I could hear the throaty hum of a car approaching. I looked out the blinds but it wasn't him. One minute past five, two minutes past five. He was late. I could have used the time to beautify myself further, but I always find the minutes after any appointment to be almost dead air. They're so deeply filled with expectation, there's no space in my mind to ask my body to do anything – or maybe I'm just a lazy arse! In any case, I was like a cat perched on a windowsill, looking out. It stressed me that there were no parking spots outside my house, and I wouldn't be able to see his car pull in. I went downstairs and hung around the hall until, through the blurry glass panels of the door, I could see the figure of him come through the gate and walk towards me.

I opened the door before he could knock.

He coolly took off his aviator sunglasses as he crossed the threshold and leant forward to give me a kiss on the cheek, baring his wide, aftershave-soaked neck to me. I took in his cargo shorts, bright red trainers, and sloganed, arthouse t-shirt. He looked youthful. A sleeve tattoo was so full of ink I couldn't make out the images. I was surprised by the breadth of his shoulders, and if that correlated to a bit of girth round his stomach it didn't matter. His pecs were bulging from his t-shirt. He reminded me of a hulking minotaur strapped into clothes.

'Come on in,' I said, leading him through to the kitchen.

'It took me a while to find your house, but I made it,' he said, and I was astonished to hear a Scottish accent. It struck me as a false note in the image I'd built up of him, as I'd been so sure he was from Belfast. A Russian accent would have sounded no more bizarre.

'Would you like tea?'

'Yeah, if you want.'

I snapped on the kettle, but when I turned back to him, he was already up close, grabbing me and kissing me so hard my head rocked back. He started to pull off my clothes. I could feel this anxiety in him, this need to make a fevered imagining real.

The kettle began to roar. We were right at the kitchen window in full view of my neighbour's landing, so I pushed him away and said 'we better go upstairs for some privacy.'

Up in the bedroom he said with a grin 'not much privacy here either,' and moved to close the blinds. He stripped down to a pair of pale blue pants covered in white stars. It made me smile that even his underwear was flamboyant. He kissed me and I felt his tight-shaved, smooth head next to mine. I flicked my tongue into the gap through his disc earring.

I could hear the hushing of the spring leaves though the open window, and it was as though they were quietening the world for us.

His right hand worked on me, his fingers quivering delicately as though on a guitar string. His other hand was on my pelvis, pinning it down, then he switched to grabbing my arm, then pushed my legs too far over my head, so that my spine was impossibly curved, and I had to wriggle out like a wrestler out of a submission hold. I wanted to cry out, but I was too excited by the unpredictability of the roughness, anticipating his next move and countering it. Then the huge span of his hand started shaking me, my thighs, my ass, my stomach, my whole body was shuddering, animated and alive, and he moaned too in unison with me.

As he clambered on top, I could feel his weight between my thighs.

'Are you alright?' he checked.

'Yes,' I said, even though I was crushed.

He kept searching my eyes, looking for some answer or connection. He looked to be suffering. 'Oh, Cora,' he murmured soulfully.

He was already inside me when I mentioned maybe we should use a condom. He didn't seem keen and I let it go.

My muscles inside squeezed him.

'Don't,' he said. 'Or I'll come.'

We lay still for a while. The wind ran through the blinds like a pianist practising scales.

'Why did you change your mind?' he whispered.

'Because I believed what you said and I wanted you to come over.'

I felt him twitch inside me and he was reanimated and moving, kissing me with his sweet and sour lips. The wind stirred the leaves again, making them sound like the pages turning in a thousand books. The skin round his neck turned a rich, goosebumpy puce.

When he came I could feel the fullness of his viscid sperm. I slipped out from beneath him and reached for a tissue. There was a small stain of rose pink in the shape of a heart left in the centre of the tissue, and I was glad to see it as it meant I wouldn't get pregnant.

We started to get dressed. I teetered around, feeling that light-headed, light-legged gravity born from entering another body's orbit. I almost felt I could float away.

We went down to the kitchen where I made some tea. I mentioned the day all those years ago when he stood on the stairs, smiling down at me, but there was a blankness on his face. As usual I was investing the past with too much significance.

'Ah, Club Biscuit, haven't seen these in years,' Leo smiled.

'How old are you?' I asked.

'Forty two,' he said. I'd thought him younger.

He told me about his new job working in security at George Best Airport.

'See? Families with children pass through my hands every day,' he said, 'so how could I have ever committed that crime? I'd never have passed the security check otherwise.'

He was still embittered at his former boss.

'Four years I'd worked there and he wouldn't believe me. You know what really got me? He even removed me from photos of staff parties on Facebook.'

He sat opposite me, a little defeated, his head sunk deep into his neck like it was a bird's roosting. I thought about how much I longed to paint him, but it would keep for another day.

'I'd better go,' he said, once his tea was drained.

I went with him out to the hall.

'Well, fun was certainly had!' I said, and he laughed and squeezed my bum.

'I'll see you soon,' he said with the hint of a question mark.

'You will.'

I stayed at the door after I'd waved him off in his car. The sun was lowering, pulling my eyes towards it as if following an actor's blazing exit. I was ecstatic, like I'd just undergone a rebirth, a re-embodiment. When I went back to the bathroom, I noticed a livid red mark just above my collarbone. I hadn't had a love bite in about fifteen years and the sight of it irritated me.

It was only later in the black liquorice night that I woke up with a start. The trees outside were hissing sibilantly in the wind, the chimney mournfully lowing, and I thought again of the twelve-year-old girl. What if? Even after sharing our bodies I still didn't know him. Wasn't that a childish act, giving me a love bite? He'd never once said he didn't like young girls, that the idea disgusted him. Maybe he was all bright on the outside, and dark, dark, dark within. And his eyes? His eyes had told me nothing.

And the thing was, half of me didn't care. I was just relieved and delighted I'd had sex.

YOU AND THE BRITBABES

The final straw comes when the dole have insisted you get reskilled, and have drafted you onto an office training course, otherwise known as 'monkeys can type too'. It is your first morning there and the woman who runs it is conducting a simulated business exercise called 'how to answer the telephone'. When it comes to your turn, you find it very disconcerting that you are sitting five metres away from her and you can see and hear her perfectly without use of the telecommunication medium. You think it's amusing to make up a company called The Girl-U-Like Escort Agency; she does not. A violently bitter argument ensues between you about the grammatical merits of 'may I help you' as opposed to 'can'.

You decide then and there you are not going back.

That night in your flat you formulate your new career move. You think of some of the most important women in the British economy. You look at yourself in the mirror. Fortunately, it is only a small hand mirror and you are spared the full effect of yourself. But you do think you have some potential.

You have been reading in recent weeks about the reported rift in the Spice Girls' ranks and you are ready to exploit it.

Now you know what you must do. The next day, you track down Posh Spice's ex-boyfriend to a small flat in Sheffield which he shares with two shaggy, indeterminate dogs. At first he doesn't seem interested because he is engrossed in watching the Teletubbies, but you impress on him the fact that Posh Spice, or Victoria, is desperately unhappy with her life. Her footballer hasn't turned out the perfect match for her. You tell him you know that deep inside she wants him back because he was the only one who truly loved her for what she once was.

There are tears in his eyes. He will rescue her, he vows, as he runs to get packed.

You haven't told him that the management could be about to ditch her anyway because she is the Boring Spice and she keeps buying dresses from Harvey Nics and generally maintaining a style which is beyond the fiscal capacities of her six-year-old fans, but that doesn't seem important.

A few days later, the tabloids and even the broadsheets (such is the Spice Girls' fame) announce that Posh Spice is leaving the band to marry her unemployed brickie ex-boyfriend.

Phase two of the plan immediately goes into action. You get on a train down to London and go straight to the Spice Girls' offices. I've come to be the new Spicer, you tell two guys. One is besuited, the other looks like he would be more at home picking cockles off a windswept beach.

'What's your image, then?' they ask you, unexpectedly. You thought they, being the image-makers, would take care of all that.

'Brainy Spice,' you say, as it's the first thing that comes into your head, and you waffle something you think appropriate about the patriarchal view of women in history and sisters doing it for themselves.

Mid-sentence, you notice they have this look on their faces like you've just endorsed Germaine Greer's views on the vasectomisation of men.

'We already have a Scary Spice,' they say to you, perplexed, and suddenly you know you should have said Fluffy Spice, so you say it as an alternative.

'Funky Spice,' shouts out the suited guy, mishearing you. 'That's exactly what we're looking for. Have you got any cool sayings?'

'Shag everything in sight ... steal everything that isn't nailed to the floor ... don't take drugs, just sell them.' You hope these are something along the right lines, but the two guys aren't even listening anymore.

'Great, fantastic fresh attitude,' says the cockle-picker guy. 'I see you already in a silver plunge back jumpsuit.'

'And I see you in a white jacket with the sleeves sewn up,' you tell him.

'No, I see her in paisley myself,' says the suited guy.

'I was thinking more of LA myself,' you say.

Glancing out the window it looks like you have just made it in time, because by now there is a queue of nevergonnabes who have the same idea as you stretching round the building three times.

You are sent down the corridor where you are orthodontically and epidermally analysed by a council of style consultants. Fortunately, you look quite young for age thirty. You have always attributed this to the rejuvenating effects of alcohol. One of the women scribbles this theory down onto her notepad.

So you join the monster rich pop princesses and you start travelling the world on a transatlantic tide of oestrogen. Life is an endless whirl of film sets, TV studios and award nights. Your persona of Funky Spice is an instant hit and you are voted number one in the popularity poll. This does cause a frisson of jealousy within the group, particularly from Sporty who is condemned to wear Adidas and always comes last in the popularity stakes, so much so that during dance practice she directs a couple of her speciality high kicks in the direction of your head. But you milk your pizzazzy popularity to the full. In your meeting with Prince Charles, however, you do go a bit far when you ask if you can see his crown jewels and make bad taste innuendos about Buck-King-ham Palace and the royal wee. Your management hauls you in and tells you that the mint sauce of royalty doesn't like to be spiced up. You personally think Charles quite liked it. This is not the first time you have been warned to watch your step. It doesn't escape your notice that laid out on your bed every morning over the next week are sets of the tackiest, most risible clothes on the market.

Part of your new job consists of trotting off answers for those endless fanzines. You enjoy this. Years of playing at making up your own answers are now paying off (*sic*):

> Top Tip: Never fill your hot water bottle when you are pissed.
> Pet Hate: Hamster.
> Hate: Hairdressers that have big windows onto the street, so that you can be spotted wearing a perm cap.
> Least liked comment: If only I was twenty years younger, love
> ...
> Best answer: So what? I'd still be single and you'd still be an ugly bastard.

In fact, everything is going so well, it is a shock when you are asked if you can sing. You certainly can't dance, so you are surprised that they think you might sing. They are arranging an a cappella performance during a press conference to prove we can sing live. You are rushed to remedial singing lessons, but after five days you still sound like a bronchitic budgerigar. By the time the press conference comes round, you have been advised to mime and let the others do the singing. Straight into the song, there's this terrible drone and for a second you wonder if it is you, but to your relief it's coming from Baby Spice. It would be kind to her to say her singing voice resembles that of a spiritualist possessed by the soul of a Native American chief. The press members are so dazed it takes minutes for them to recover themselves and ask us questions. The first question goes to Scary Spice: Any plans for you and Eric Cantona to settle down?

'No, no,' laughs Scary. 'We're just having some fun at the moment. At my age I'm not into ... what's that word that sounds like a type of wood ... I forget ...'

'Mahogany,' you say, trying to help her out. But for the life of you, you cannot remember the word she means. It worries you. For the rest of the interview you are uncustomarily quiet.

You and the girls go back to your hotel. Truth be told, you are getting rather bored with their company. Scary is sitting on the edge of the bed, thinking up dynamic slogans such as 'reach for the top' and 'go do it, girls'. It's what they call soundbites, she says. Sounds shite is more the term for it, you mutter under your breath. She is contemplating going into politics with her campaign based on 'I've better hair than Tony Blair'. You don't think someone who thinks an ECU is a bird with a long neck would be ideally suited to run the country, but after all it is up to her.

Ginger Spice is busy body-stencilling to see if she would look good in a full body tattoo, and Baby Spice is sewing gingham shelf trims for her mother. How little you have in common with them. Sporty suggests going to visit Robbie Williams in his detox centre and you decide to tag along. Because the hotel is surrounded by hundreds of iconolatrous fans, you have to slide out the window on a zip cord which leads down to a warehouse housing your private limo. You wonder what the distinction is between a groupie and an insane stalker. They all look seriously deranged to you.

One day there is a tiny piece in the paper about how Victoria Posh Adams has just had a baby girl. We are near the end of our whistle stop live world tour and, amazingly, people now seem to like our new, punky out-of-tune style better than our bland version. Even serious artists like Neneh Cherry and Sheryl Crow are saying hi to us at award ceremonies. We're slowly becoming more herbal resin than bubblegum.

The news about Posh Spice has an extraordinary effect. Ginger Spice phones her up and finds out how happy she is with her new life. Before you know it, Ginger starts to get maudlin and says how she wishes she could be a normal person again. Then Sporty says 'do you remember playing football on a Sunday afternoon and then having a few pints and some chips afterwards?' Nobody does, but each is suddenly lost in her rosy memories of the past. All four charter a plane to Sheffield to visit the baby spicelet. Meanwhile, you stay in America leading your noctilucent lifestyle and you go out briefly with an astronaut who's famous for probing the stars.

The next day, you discover the papers are full of the girls' announcement that they are splitting up. You have not been consulted. Sporty, Scary, Ginger and Baby are going back to their old boyfriends to lead the simple life. They say they are tired of living out of a suitcase (you think being accompanied by a travelling wardrobe of five hundred items of clothing hardly constitutes lugging a suitcase around) and they have been living a hollow sham without family and friends. They now realise they have been untrue to one of their founding maxims: Be true to yourself.

You are horrified. You insist on being hooked up to them live by satellite. 'Are you out of your tiny gourds?'

you ask them. 'We've got a good thing going here. Ok, so we'll have a shelf life no longer than Paul Newman's salad dressing, but let's cash in while we can. What do you say, Ginge?'

'My name's Geri, not Ginger,' she says, and her eyes seem even more vacuous than before if that's possible. She seems inordinately happy that she can go back to her old mousy brown colour.

'Big deal. The wages of freedom are very low,' you remind them. 'And what about our anthem, *Wannabe*? It was about how men could come and go but the group would always stick together. Did we sell that as a lie to millions of children around the world?' You start singing the bit about *yougottagetwithmyfriends* and *friendshipneverends*.

One by one, they stand up and leave. 'You never could sing,' says Baby.

You are left staring into the Spiceless screen. You start shouting, hoping one of them might hear you. 'GIRLPOWER! BE WHAT YOU WANNA BE! SHAKE IT MOVE IT MAKE IT FAKE IT SHOW THEM HOW GOOD YOU ARE! YOU HAVE GOT THE POWER!' And as you shout, you almost believe it, but you are also thinking how long it will take you to spend what's in your account and you figure your best move is to phone Bananarama and see if they want to make a comeback.

PORTRAIT OF A EUROPEAN CITY

Painting White No 6

Freya McConnell was in charge of regenerating East Belfast. As she cycled down the Newtownards Road she wished with a laugh she could regenerate her own senescent twinges. To her left were the old Sirocco Works, now converted into offices, and the brand new budget hotel made up of shipping containers. She'd pilfered that idea from the container hotels spotted on her Airbnb breaks in Berlin and Amsterdam – all part of her grand plan to transform Belfast.

The statue of the C.S. Lewis lion was burning brightly in the sun. Passing the EastSide Arts Centre she waved at the barista bringing coffees to a couple sitting outside. She was disappointed to see the mural of famous cultural alumni already beginning to fade and flake in the light. Recently two of those alumni had died, but new writers and artists were on the rise everywhere. That very morning, she'd confided to a friend that the cultural renaissance was almost too vibrant now; too many books and posters of artwork for the EastSide Café to stock. At this rate of going, there would be a blue plaque on every street corner.

She turned past Connswater Shopping Centre and Avoniel. The houses along the Albertbridge Road had broken out in paint blisters, and weeds were proliferating from the walls and the mouths of chimney pots. Empty tobacco packets, scratch cards and prescription strips were being nudged along the pavements by the breeze. Of course, the main aim of enculturing the east was to bring the 'more problematic' areas along with it, showing them an alternative to gunmen, murals, flutes and flags, but progress was slow.

She glanced right at the Templemore Baths which was now an art gallery, another of her pet projects. An aroma of pizza blasted out from an air vent. At the traffic lights she noticed a mattress dumped down an alley with burst bags of rubbish and she caught a whiff of urine that made her wince. As she cycled under the 'I Support Soldier F' flags in their magisterial maroon and royal reds, she couldn't help but cringe. They were beating overhead, making a sound that reminded her of windbreaks on the shore.

Painting Black No 9
Freya chained her bike to the lamp post outside Woodstock Library. The library's narrow windows suggested a shy reluctance to promote books amidst a street of thriving beauty salons, kebab houses and vaping shops. The poster advertising today's arts exhibition was curling inwards from its own lack of confidence.

Freya walked through to a brightly-lit, white-walled room. She was delighted to see a crowd had gathered – the usual wealthy retirees, some aspiring artists, directors from other festivals, and, encouragingly, a smattering of Woodstock locals. They were helping themselves to the cheap, red launch wine, one man joking it was so vinegary you could pour it over your chips. The room was also peppered with critics, bloggers and social media influencers busy tapping and snapping. The artist, Danny Fitzsimons, was renowned for spending as much time curating his guest list as his art.

'Hey ya, Freya,' said Danny, kissing her on the cheek. His lips had already purpled from the wine. 'Great news, Bernadette Agnew is on her way over. She just texted me.'

'Are you sure about that?' Freya checked.

'But I told you she'd accepted my invitation.'

'Yeah, but she's well known for accepting every invitation going and never actually turning up.'

'You don't seem very keen. I thought you'd be delighted someone that high profile is coming.'

'I just wished you'd confirmed it earlier,' she said, trying to tone down her dismay. 'Though I'm sure it'll be fine.'

It was normal to ask permission from the local community reps whenever a contentious figure attended a function in their district, but it was far too late to do anything about it now. She shrugged to herself and picked up one of the canapés topped with a gelatinous paste she guessed was pâté.

She was taking her launch speech out of her bag when Bernadette Agnew, Sinn Féin MLA, breezed in, accompanied by a cameraman. Bernadette Agnew was typical of politicians in that she never walked – she whirled in or she strutted; every movement was a big show, a power play. She was talking to the camera as it rolled, pointing extravagantly to the art work.

Freya went over to her.

'Freya!' Bernadette exclaimed, reaching out for her hand. 'Thank you for inviting me.'

Freya couldn't let it pass. 'Well, officially it was Danny, but you're very welcome here.'

'Hope you don't mind, but I'm filming a few shots of the exhibition – just a few clips we'll use exclusively for promoting our own Féile. I wanted to give coverage to the cutting-edge artists venturing into the east.'

'Venturing', Freya noted, as if it was into a hostile territory.

'That's absolutely fine, Bernadette. We're always delighted to showcase how the east is more open than the rest of Belfast to all colours and creeds.'

Got you back, exulted Freya.

'Though there are no colours here,' Bernadette rejoindered with a smile, wafting her hand expansively round the austere white and black paintings relieved by the occasional microdot of colour. Their message was implicit; communities needed to transcend their old allegiances to tribal colours.

Painting White with Green Spot No 12

Later that evening, Freya carried a box out onto the decking at the bottom of the garden. From its raised position, she could see her neighbours catch the last of the evening sun, reclining in their chairs like they were on a long-haul flight. She sat down next to the deep red hydrangea bush and lit some lemongrass candles to ward off the midgies. She opened the box, telling herself it was fourteen months since that day, and it was time Lola's room stopped feeling like a storage space in a mausoleum.

On top was a postcard: 'Hi Mum, as you can see, I'm in Sofia ...' She already felt the wet blur in her eyes and threw it into the 'to be discarded' pile without reading any further. The only way she could do this was by being ruthless. She took out Lola's old library card, then realised it was such a pretty photo, she'd have to keep it. But what was the point of keeping anything? No one else would be interested but her, and yet it felt so wrong to ditch these traces of Lola's life, almost as if she was desecrating a memorial. Next up was one of Lola's school reports and she scanned down the column of As, marred by one solitary C in Maths, together with the teacher's exhortation for Lola to 'apply herself'. 'Bitch,' she said, reliving the outrage of twenty years ago.

It had been a sudden collapse in a bar. A late-night call from Lola's boyfriend, Jack, to say Lola had been taken by ambulance to the hospital where ER staff were trying to revive her. He'd call back as soon as he had any news. For the next hour she dashed round the house, pulling out her suitcase, throwing in her clothes, looking up flights to London on her phone. Then the sobbing call from Jack to say the consultants had done what they could, but it had been a massive heart attack. She was so young it didn't seem possible. For weeks, Freya kept shouting out a long, keening 'no' of disbelief to the world. She found that friends and relatives stayed away out of fear of upsetting her, but it felt as if she'd committed some scandal for which she was being punished.

Freya was just consigning the report to the discarded pile when a text came through from a member of the EastBel Arts board, telling her to check Bernadette Agnew's Twitter account. 'It isn't good,' the text concluded. She quickly looked it up and found a clip of Bernadette charging into the Woodstock Library, quoting the words of Bobby Sands:

> The Men of Art have lost their heart,
> They dream within their dreams.
> Their magic sold for price of gold
> Amidst a people's screams.

Bernadette went on to say that Danny's new exhibition was full of heart and was challenging the prevailing political beliefs and bigotry of the east. Freya's hands flew up to her face. Oh, fuck, it was a major balls-up and she was going to have to make a grovelling admittance of error to every board member. She couldn't believe that Bernadette Agnew, knowing how feelings ignited every summer, was trying to make political capital out of this. The barefaced cheek of her to claim she'd only been filming for the Féile, but you couldn't expect a fair fight from the likes of an ex-IRA bomber, could you?

It was time to make some calls. She closed up the box and blew out the candles, noticing the shadows of the hedges stretching around her. Next door's recliners were empty. She carried the box inside and was about to throw the discarded remnants of Lola's life into the recycling bins when she realised she wasn't ready. She'd need to give herself more time.

Painting White with Orange Spot No 13
The mobile was ringing beside her bed. Freya's eyes sprung open and she sat up as she answered, trying to shake the sleep out of her voice.

'Hello?'

'Freya, Alex here. I had to get to you before the press does.'

Alex was one of the board members. Overnight, Alex told her, bricks had smashed the glass door of Woodstock Library. Tommy Robb, the UVF leader, was apparently furious that Bernadette Agnew had walked into his district without him knowing a thing of it.

'Ok, Alex, I'll draft a statement right now from EastBel Arts.'

8.15am it was. She'd deliberately allowed herself a lie-in after being up half the night, her mind racing about Lola. She ran downstairs to put the kettle on. That call was like a cold shower on her head. While the kettle bubbled, she switched on her laptop, moving fast. The last thing she wanted was for the EastSide Arts Centre to be targeted.

Another call came through from the festival programmer and she sought to downplay the whole situation – 'a show of power from Robb and a few other backward-thinking mesomorphs', she designated it. An apology to the local community would soon smooth it over. She remembered how Lola had once sneaked off to an anti-war demo during school and she'd saved her from suspension by writing a speedy apology to the principal. 'Mum, you're the best bacon-saver in the world,' Lola had said at the time.

Freya composed a quick email to the board, foisting most of the blame for the incident onto the deserving shoulders of Danny Fitzsimons, then pressed send. She'd just started on a press release when a new email pinged back from Danny.

'I realise inviting Bernadette has caused trouble,' he said, 'and I'm very sorry to hear about it, but I think it's a case that I was more naïve than "irresponsible".'

Christ, thought Freya, realising she'd cc'd Danny in by accident. She scrolled down, panicking at what else she'd written. She could easily have referred to his overweening obsession with inviting the rich and influential to his exhibitions, but luckily she'd held back on this occasion. Still, she was more prone to making mistakes these days, and Lola would have rolled her eyes. Lola ... Outside, she could hear the dry summer leaves shiver and jostle and almost jingle against each other in the wind. Cypresses, beeches, sycamores – trees that had lived for a hundred years or more. Above the trees, the rumpled, flocculent sky resembled an unmade bed. Come on, she told herself – this wasn't the moment to be distracted, and she had to fight to save her own bacon. She went back to the press release and began typing and rephrasing, typing and rephrasing ...

Painting Black with Black Spot No 16
Freya turned and twisted in front of the full-length mirror. Her dark jacket was sober, indicating the gravity of the situation – '*très* profesh' she told herself, pushing her shoulders back as she viewed herself, front, side and back.

Tommy Robb had refused to be mollified by the statement appearing in *The Belfast Telegraph* and *The Newsletter*, and was demanding a full explanation, so Freya had decided the only way forward was to hold a public meeting at the local community centre on the Mount.

She thought about hopping on the Glider, another of the local success stories she'd backed, but she was running out of time and the sky had a heavy grey belly. Its waters broke just as she pulled out the drive, but by the time she reached Templemore, the sun was inching its way out again. She was struck by the beauty of two tiny rainbows appearing in the spray spumed from the wheels of the car in front.

The Glider was sliding down the Albertbridge Road, reminding her of her multiple broken promises to use it. Just so no one would know she'd driven, she decided not to park anywhere near the community centre. She found a space next to a bit of waste ground full of woodbine, spotted laurel and bramble, making a mental note that it needed developing. The pavements were wildly undulating, the orange leaves floating in puddles like dead, belly-up fish.

The community centre reminded her of a building on an industrial park; one of those small-windowed affairs built towards the end of the Troubles, she observed. She slowly sucked in the air to settle herself. At the door, the DUP MLA, Johnny Turkington, shook hands with her and made a sympathetic face. Alex from the board was waiting at reception, but she whispered 'go you on in first, then I'll come.' If there was one thing she'd learnt over the years it was that arriving in a group made your enemies attack all the more ferociously. The trick was to look vulnerable.

As she made her way into the hall, she could see Tommy Robb sitting imposingly on his own in the centre of the front row, arms crossed. He had two sleeve tattoos covering up the old prison etchings. She knew how he'd ended up in prison; who didn't? He was notorious for the murder years ago of Hammy McCord. He'd parked his car opposite Hammy's girlfriend's house and had lain in the back seat for three days under some blankets, pissing in jars. Finally, when Hammy showed up, Tommy jumped out with a machine gun and shot him dead. He was nothing if not tenacious.

Down in the audience, a journalist from *The Newsletter* was impatiently tapping her fingers on her pen like it was a flute. Freya stepped up on to the stage alone and felt the hall hush.

'I've invited you all here today as, like you, I'm aghast at the occurrences of the past few days. Let me just add that the artist, Danny Fitzsimons, who staged his exhibition as a peace and reconciliation event, deeply regrets the negative impact it has caused, and especially the hurt visited on the local community ...'

Tommy Robb got up and walked loudly out of the hall. Freya blinked in surprise and then carried on.

Painting White with Blood Spot No 17
Two afternoons later, Freya turned into Templemore Avenue. The closer she came to Tommy Robb's house, the more flags there were. The traffic slowed down as police in neon lime jackets waved it to a halt. Was it an accident, Freya wondered. Within seconds she could hear the pound of a drum, followed by ear-piercing flutes, signalling it was just a local feeder band making its way to some parade or other. As she sat in her car, children dashed through the traffic to watch. It occurred to her how tough life must be round these parts – the kids seemed to have permanent scowl lines by the age of twelve.

A stocky man passed by, flaying away at the goat hide of the Lambeg drum, its whiteness vibrating, full of dimpling like cellulite on a fat woman's thigh. Even with her car windows closed she could feel the drum beat in her chest. It was so loud you had to be drunk to bear it. Some teenage girls in sparse clothing cheered, wearing so much bronzer on their faces they seemed to have been sprayed with gold paint.

Shortly after the public meeting, Freya had discovered why Tommy Robb had left. His sixteen-year-old daughter, Shannon, had been found dead in a flat of a suspected drug overdose. It was shocking, horrible. Not only was it right for Freya to pay her respects at Tommy's house, but it would double up as a chance to say something placatory about the art exhibition *débâcle*.

She pulled up outside a simple red-brick terraced house in Castlereagh Street and knocked on the front door. Up above, the sun was crowbarring itself through a crack in the cloud. An elderly woman in a white t-shirt answered.

'Very sorry to hear of your trouble. Would Tommy be in?'

'Come on in, love,' said the woman. 'I'm Granny Annie. Tommy!' she guldered up the stairs. 'You're wanted!'

Granny Annie led her into the living room. It was conjoined to a dining area where the coffin was sitting resting on the table, the lid removed. Freya tried to avert her eyes.

'Did you know Shannon?' Granny Annie asked.

'No, sorry, I didn't.'

'This is her and her sister from years ago,' Granny Annie said, pointing to the images on her t-shirt. 'But their faces have fattened out a bit over the years, eh?' she laughed lightly, poking fun at the largeness of her own breasts. 'Would you take a wee cuppa, love?'

'No thanks.'

Granny Annie went out into the hall to shout up for Tommy again. Freya noticed a letter from the council sitting on a unit and couldn't resist a sneaky look. 'We called today', it said, 'because of reports that you haven't been using your recycling boxes ...'

She pulled away from it as Tommy came in.

'Hello, Freya,' said Tommy, shaking her hand. 'Thanks for coming.'

'Not at all. I heard what had happened after the meeting. So sorry for your loss.'

'Come and meet Shannon,' said Tommy, leading her over to the coffin.

Shannon was thin and delicate, in a long blue satin dress and a white fur jacket, her shoes beaded, like she was going to her high school formal. Her hands lay across her stomach as though smoothing down her dress. There was something stately about her, almost Disney princess. Her hair was a lustrous black, but just at the side of her temple a faint bruise was lurking beneath the first follicles, and Freya wondered if she'd fallen as she died, if she'd hurt herself somehow. Tommy was rubbing his fingers along the pine edge of the coffin, like he wanted to reach in and stir her.

Freya felt her legs shake; the smell of polish from the brass handles sickened her. A memory flashed into her mind of being twelve years old, seeing her own dad in the coffin and her mother pulling at her hand, telling her to touch him. 'He won't bite,' her mother had said, trying to harden her to the reality of death. When Lola had been brought back to Belfast, the undertaker had asked Freya if she wanted to bring her home for a wake or to visit her in the funeral parlour, but she'd said no. Coffins had always made her shiver. In the late seventies there had been those 'creepy coffin bank' money boxes where a skeletal hand crept out and snatched the coin away. Besides, she wanted to remember Lola full of life, not dead, wanted to remember the first moment she saw her as a newborn, not the last as a corpse.

'I thought seeing her would make me accept it more, but it doesn't,' said Tommy, staring in at Shannon. There was the lightest tremble in his lips. 'Just sixteen years of age.'

Freya reached out and touched his arm.

'I lost my daughter too, just over a year ago. She was thirty four.'

'Does it get better?'

'Yes, it does,' she said with conviction, but she could feel a lie in her words.

She wanted to leave but couldn't take her eyes away.

'She's beautiful,' she said, but it was almost to fill the space.

The girl's eyelids were a tiny bit sunken, her skin too waxy under the makeup, her jaw a little too deeply set to seem fully human.

Granny Annie led a newly-arrived teenager to the coffin. Freya moved back as Tommy shook his hand. It was strange, this old Irish ritual of everyone coming to see the body. Come and ride the ghost train. Choo choo! Hop on the night express to Deadwood! What was it with this country? Were people so childish here that they didn't believe death was real until they saw it face-to-face? Surely Tommy of all people knew exactly what death was.

'The human body is all space and vibrations,' someone had once told her. That was what the physicists said, but there was something more than air and quivering flesh. There was some element of magic. She noticed how the wooden hexagonal lid was propped up against the wall like a narrow door tapering towards the top and she imagined it as some otherworldly portal into a secret realm.

Freya turned to go, but Tommy called out to her.

'I'd like a word with you,' he said, taking her into the hall. 'About Bernadette Agnew. It's not that I mind her coming east at all, but if I don't hear of it first, I lose face in the community.'

'I totally understand that,' said Freya. 'I would have told you, only I didn't know till it was too late. But attacking the library was wrong too.'

'Sometimes the community can't express things in words.'

'The community needs to, Tommy.'

'Lose face, you put the balaclava on, you have to. It's the law here.'

'Illegality is the law?'

He looked at her in frustration.

'Come out with me,' he said and she followed him into the sun.

He nodded across at the new apartment block called The Bank. 'You see? You think you're so perfect, but all your developments mean is we don't have a bank here anymore.' He pointed down the road to another new block. 'The Bakery, see? You and all your crusades, you've stripped us of all our amenities.'

'The bank and bakery wanted to close.'

'Aye, but you made it easy for them.'

'You don't object when it suits you,' said Freya, lowering her voice. 'Sure I built you your museum.'

'Only 'cause you want to consign us to the past.'

People were passing by. He barely moved his lips in the manner of someone used to telling secrets.

'You think you can shape the east and get rid of us, when deep down you know you'd be nowhere without us. You can despise me but without us fighting back all those years, there would have been a United Ireland and you wouldn't have your top job, amn't I right?'

'No matter who has my job, Tommy, the city has to change.'

'Change isn't always good.'

A vague image of Lola flitted across her mind.

She shook his hand and left. His words stung her somewhat, but people were so used to fighting over land here they couldn't see how great that land could be. As she went back to her car she saw a bulldozer sitting down a side road, its huge open maw ready to gobble up more ancient bricks and history. As she drove off, she passed yet another JCB behind a makeshift fence. Its teeth ground on the earth and let out a sudden painful ululation. She almost jumped the light to get away, then swung onto Templemore, trying to block out the scrakes and the hammering of the new builds. She looked up to the sky for relief. Up above, the royal reds, maroons, regal blues and flaunting oranges flapped and danced in the August breeze.

THE NIGHT THEY SHOT THE JOURNALIST

The sun was still shining, its orange eye peering out between the top of the Creggan and a ridge of cloud. Morgan was heading home from town, thinking how neon the green, white and gold bunting looked in the sun's glow, when he passed the bonfire. Just then, he noticed something new about it. Something wrong.

The internment bonfire was on an overgrown piece of waste ground, accessed by a torn-down gap in the fencing. A billboard promising new social housing had been turned back to front with the words 'Wood Only – No Dumping' scrawled across it. As if in mockery of the developers, the only housing thus far was a ramshackle lookout hut for the kids.

Morgan strode over to the bonfire, taking in the details of the wooden murals round its base. Each mural showed an image from the history of the Protestant people in Derry (or Londonderry as they called it) – besieged behind the walls, emigrating on ships, joining the civil rights march ... Only two weeks ago, these boards had been erected on a wall beside the Fountain Estate to a huge fanfare of local councillors extolling the virtues of cross-community tolerance.

'Who put these here?' Morgan asked one of the kids in the hut. None of the teenagers were around.

'I don't know, mate,' said the kid.

Mate, Morgan noted indignantly, but let it go.

He pulled the murals off and stacked them. There were five and they looked heavier than he'd first calculated but surely he'd be able to make it to his house, two streets away. He lifted them up, feeling the weight of them right down into his knees, the long, low gurn of his muscles. Maybe it was karma, the way he was beginning to have trouble with his knees.

He staggered along the road with his strange cargo past the church, polystyrene burger cartons impaled on its railings. The road was full of fast food shops and beauty salons. He was always alert to the irony that one made you fat while the other made you beautiful. There were more nail bars than real bars these days.

As soon as he reached his front garden, he threw the murals down in relief. He then took each one into his backyard where he stacked them against his wall. He wondered about repercussions, and if he should tape up his letterbox, but surely the bonfire builders had so much wood they would hardly care.

A couple in a neighbouring house were talking fast in a language he couldn't understand. Ever since Una and Lorcan had moved out he'd tuned into the voices around him. He often imagined that the newcomers were discussing some secret complex philosophy when all they were probably saying was 'pass the ketchup'. That was how his own fascination with Irish had begun in prison, engendered by the idea it could teach him things beyond the narrow reach of English.

He took a chair outside, enjoying the cooling of the night air. The sky had already darkened into dusk when he saw one last lone bird fly swiftly across its vastness. It was odd, as if it had stayed out late, partied too long, missed the last bus back.

He was lying on the sofa an hour later watching a film on Netflix when a heavy rap sounded on his door. He got up, guessing it meant trouble.

Five teenage boys were crowding his front door.

'Give us our murals back,' one of them demanded. Morgan knew his name was Seán Óg, knew him for being mouthy.

'No. You're not getting them back.' He tried to sound as authoritative as possible, drawing himself up on his toes. 'And here's why. They're cultural murals. They mean stuff to the Protestants. Only scumbags would burn them. You don't destroy their culture.'

'Sure they don't have a fucking culture,' fired back Seán Óg.

He could see their eyes sizing him up, taking in how, at fifty, he was broader than them and looked handy.

'Yes, they do. Look, I don't give a fuck what you put on the bonfire,' he said, roughening his voice. 'Union Jacks, DUP posters, knock yourself out, but you're not getting them murals back. Because it's wrong. That's not what we fought for, to stamp on their culture.'

'We don't give a fuck what you fought for. This is now and we're the fighters.'

'This is the way it is, lads. Goodnight to you.'

He shut the door firmly on them. He could hear their cursing through the rim of the door, through the plastic letterbox. He held his breath till the creak of the gate told him they were away. His former IRA days didn't win him any glory with the new breed. Eyes like those would strip the medals off your chest if you'd had them, but he was glad he'd held his ground. The teenagers looked slight in their skinny jeans and fitted t-shirts but the danger was they didn't know any fear.

After a minute, he opened the door again. The street was empty but for a black cat slinking along. It paused and stared at him with its silver-star eyes.

The next morning he was up early, making phone calls, arranging interviews. He'd been commissioned by TG4 to make two Irish language documentaries, one on Ulster Scots and the other on vampire folklore. The filming for both had to be wrapped up by autumn and it was going to be tight. It was also on his mind to phone the City Council and inform them about the murals, but he told himself he was too busy right now and it would keep.

At lunchtime he walked down the road to visit his cameraman, Jim, for a chat. As he passed the bonfire, he caught sight through the buddleia of two teenagers from the night before sitting on the back of a sofa. They were yawning like lions who'd just feasted. An old phrase his granny used to say uncomfortably drifted into his mind: if you burn your arse, you'll have to sit on the blister.

Peadar Ó Mhichil was walking up the opposite side of the street. Peadar deliberately looked the other way, but Morgan watched him head through the fencing to the bonfire. Peadar had his hooks into those boys, thought Morgan, but what had he done in the Troubles? Sweet Fuck All, except for composing a song they sometimes sang in the GAA and working men's clubs, and you'd have thought he was Dominic Behan the way he still milked it. The Derry Provies had talked loads, but done little. Most of the action had gone down in Belfast, and all Peadar was known for was agitating at Orange parades. Peadar in turn had always resented the fact that Morgan was a big-man blow-in from Belfast and teased him about it in public, pretending it was a bit of friendly slagging rather than a blatant diminution.

Outside Jim's house, Morgan checked his phone for reports about the missing murals. Right enough there was a mention of it in a BBC news tweet. In some way it thrilled him to have stolen goods in his backyard. It had been so many years, what, thirty or more, since he'd stashed something, but he still had misgivings about riling the teenagers. He suddenly remembered Una saying she was starting a cross-community group for teenagers from the Creggan and the Waterside. He could dander into the town this evening to see if the boys were there, and maybe use it to chat to Una too. He and Una were now at the point where they could look each other in the eye. There was no warmth yet but it was the start of a rapprochement. It was mad to him that after serving on so many reconciliation committees he and his wife had ended up with a gulf as big as a sectarian divide.

The community centre was brand spanking new, the walls covered in murals of children from all different ethnic backgrounds playing together. It was hard, mused Morgan, not to think you were being brainwashed in multiculturalism; even the most modern buildings that were supposedly neutral wore their political colours.

He went up a stairway that had the smell of a hospital and turned into a corridor full of small conference rooms – 'Meeting Room' each was called on the door, and he stifled a laugh at how everything was rebranded to sound friendly. One of the doors was open and Una was standing inside next to tables stacked with pizza boxes, packets of Tayto and barrack-busters of Coca Cola. She looked tired, he noticed, her hair dry and faded like it had been kept in an antique locket.

'Hey,' she called out, surprised to see him.

'Just popping by,' he said. 'Had a wee run in with some of the teenagers yesterday, so I thought I'd suss out the vibe.'

'No one's here yet. It's only the second week of it,' explained Una, embarrassed.

'How's Lorcan?'

'Sound as a pound.'

'But less than a fiver, eh?' quipped Morgan.

Una didn't smile and he chided himself for always trying to charm her when there was no need anymore.

'Wants to be at his daddy's riding his new bike,' said Una pointedly.

'Well, I love to have him too,' he said, defusing her comment.

The bike had been a source of contention. In Una's eyes, Morgan was luring Lorcan away from her with this bright, shiny new toy. Christ, Morgan thought, you'd think I was a child snatcher the way she got on.

Just then, a couple of teenage girls mooched in, making straight for the pizza. The sun was glowing off their skin like it had been slapped.

'So, how are things with you girls?' asked Una, delighted to see them. The brisk turn of her back told Morgan he was no longer welcome.

He muttered a goodbye and left.

Outside, two teenagers were pushing an industrial-size trolley, stacked perilously high with pallets, down the centre of the road. A trail of cars was building up behind. One of the cars tooted impatiently but the bonfire builders flipped the driver the finger before turning down the side street.

It was still stiflingly hot. Perfect rioting weather, Morgan reckoned. The sun was lowering into his vision and he made a brim with his hand. As he approached the bonfire, he could see Seán Óg standing on top, looking down at him. Conscious that it looked like he was saluting him, Morgan whipped his hand away from his eyes.

'Alright, lads?' he shouted across, sounding confident.

He could hear a few whispers and laughs, the slow *psss* of a beer can being opened, the harsh kerpluck of the ring pull. He walked on past a big chock of cow parsley poking through the fencing. The midgies were circling, phosphorescent in the light.

He was sure he could hear the words 'big man' being bandied derisively behind his back. They were still angry at him, but in the old days back in Belfast such boys would have been dealt with. Seán Óg would have been recruited, exiled or maimed. Not that Morgan had ever condoned the maiming, but sometimes you had to enforce discipline just to stop things spiraling out of control. Sure, the community was all woolly and liberal and snowflakey these days, but they had forgotten how it was back then. Even worse, they were letting these boys get a hold over them.

At home he poured himself a glass of wine and strolled through to his backyard. A long streak of bird excrement had painted itself across the murals like a vandal's handiwork. A blackbird, perhaps the very culprit, was whistling from a rooftop in such a joyful way Morgan couldn't help whistling back in imitation. Often the birds would reply, but tonight there was silence, leaving Morgan to wonder if his whistle had had an edge to it. A dog started barking, setting another one off in duet, one with the deep, stentorian bark of Pavarotti, the other a soprano. Right, he chided himself sharply. Do a bit of housework, then relax with more wine. He went into the kitchen where the day's dishes were piled up awaiting him, and started scrubbing the frying pan with an old Brillo pad. The Brillo pad made clouds of blood red in the water. He quickly rinsed it away.

He was in a deep, vinous sleep when a loud bang woke him up. He opened his bleary eyes and peered at his mobile – 23:55. Must have been a firework or a slamming door, he told himself, keeping half an ear out for any other disruption. Nothing came and he slowly let his mind fall back into the downward escalator of sleep.

'Abhartach, the vampire from north Derry who ruled in the sixth century and drank the blood of his subjects, was killed by a sword of yew wood and buried with a heavy stone laid on his chest,' read Morgan the following morning. 'Abhartach's grave still exists in Glenullin as a large stone adjacent to a hawthorn tree. In 1997 there were attempts to clear the land, but a workman who tried to cut down the hawthorn lost control of the chainsaw, cutting his hand, allowing the blood to drip into the grave ...' Wow, thought Morgan, jotting down a note to try and locate the workman for an interview. Maybe he'd give that young journalist, Ciara McCord, a ring as she was writing about the graves of Troubles victims in the area.

A text came through from Jim, his cameraman. 'Did you hear the trouble last night?'

Morgan googled 'trouble in the Creggan' and instantly a ton of pages flicked up about a gunshot in the night. He phoned Jim who reckoned the dissidents had been trying to lure in the police in order to whip up anger from the local residents. They had been upping this tactic in the Bogside too, but the police were getting wise to it now and stayed away. It seemed the dissies were acting up to an MTV camera crew who had arrived in the area to document trouble.

'Have you heard about the new training camps in Donegal?' asked Jim.

Morgan had already heard the rumours. Over thirty years ago Morgan had been to a training camp himself, living with eight other lads in a cottage in the remote lee of a mountain. He'd learnt how to shoot, how to make explosives, about republican ideals. It disturbed him that the past was all bubbling up again, but he chased it away, telling himself it was another scorcher of a day, way too bright for dark thoughts.

Besides, he had some shopping to do in town. He put away his books, put on a fresh linen shirt and went out. A new piece of graffiti had been sprayed on a wall two streets away: 'they blow up so young these days'. He couldn't help laughing out loud in spite of himself at the blackness of it.

There wasn't a soul at the bonfire, not a sound but for the buzz of insects drawn in by the wild honeysuckle and the blackberry flowers climbing up round the fence. It wouldn't be long before the teenagers put in a shift as tomorrow was the anniversary of internment. In the distance Morgan could see the tip of a huge white marquee erected for the celebrations. The city spires looked dreamy in their dustiness, the black cannons perched like snipers on Derry's walls.

On his way into the city, he thought about how tomorrow was his turn to take the wee man, how he couldn't wait to see him. He and Una looked after Lorcan week about. He'd promised to buy him an Xbox, but was worried Una would take umbrage at what she saw as another bribe. He stopped outside the gaming shop and took a look at the huge screen in the window showing an animated female soldier with impossibly long, limber thighs shooting an enemy soldier dead. As he watched it, an image flashed into his head of himself at nineteen standing in the kitchen of a Donegal cottage, wedging the nozzle of a handgun tight against a sandbag, the instructor advising him to keep his head and shoulders still as he pulled the trigger ...

He walked away from the window, telling himself Lorcan would just have to wait. Una was right; the boy had been spoilt enough. Maybe Morgan had been overcompensating for his own deprived childhood; one of five kids. It had been a running family joke that they were that poor all a burglar could steal was the candle out of the Sacred Heart.

At times the truth was Morgan shivered at Lorcan's nature. The boy couldn't bear to wait in the car when Morgan popped in somewhere for a message. It was always seatbelt off, leaping out the door, an unfettered thirst to be out in the world, a message encoded in his young body that life was short and every second was precious. Morgan had never told Una of his fear that his son would inherit his own characteristics. Five years ago files had been leaked, revealing a psychological profile on Morgan from old police interviews. It had described him as 'a natural-born fanatic' and he'd laughed it off at the time, but the bigger Lorcan grew the more those words ate at his mind.

On his way home he thought about avoiding the bonfire but he was almost mesmerised by it now. A Union Jack was flying from the top. There was an image of a victims campaigner tied to a pallet which nauseated Morgan somewhat, but he didn't dare intervene again. The teenagers were there, working hard, stacking all the loose wood round its base and moving little mounds of rubble and brick to the side. Seán Óg was barechested, a dark tattoo on his left pec, his skin sleek with sun cream. A light breeze was getting up, making the white gravel rise in floury puffs. Morgan could feel its thickness tickle his throat.

On the corner of Morgan's street, the dog rose petals were wide open, sunbathing. A tricolour hanging in an open window was gently blowing in and out like a cloth over a breathing mouth. He went into his house, his head feeling as blurred from the heat as it ever did on the drink.

Not used to the sun was all. He drank some water, noticing the sweat sparkle on his hands, then went through to his bedroom where he lay down. He turned onto his side, feeling the cool air from his nostrils on his arm, and fell into a light trancey sleep, images flicking faster round his mind than a glitterball.

When he woke up he felt much better. He made the decision to return the murals as soon as the bonfire was burnt down. In two days' time it would be a black circle, the graffiti blacked out and the tribal trouble forgotten for another year. He'd tell the council he found them randomly dumped against a wall without even mentioning the bonfire. There was no chance he'd risk touting on those boys. He could hear the exact words of the instructor all those years before: 'If any of you tout on us, we'll kidnap your sister, we'll kill your brother, we'll make your mother disappear.'

Voices were rising in the street, making him look through the blinds. His neighbours were congregating. He gave his face a quick wash, gelled down his pillow-puffed hair and ran down.

Police cars had parked outside a house fifty yards away. Officers were trailing in and out in their baggy white boiler suits.

'What's up?' Morgan asked his neighbour.

'A raid. Her name's Saoirse and she's going buck mad.'

'Must be looking for last night's gun.'

He could see this Saoirse woman remonstrating with a detective. A couple of Shinners were on the periphery trying to intervene but Peadar Ó Mhichil was already right there in the thick of things. Morgan recognised two teenagers from the bonfire lounging on the woman's wall, their backs curved like question marks.

'There'll be trouble over this,' warned another neighbour darkly. 'The dissies will have a field day.'

Morgan went back inside. He remembered the time years ago he'd kept a gun stashed in his backyard in Belfast under the oil tank. The OC had wanted him to drive out to the country and kneecap a teenager himself, but he'd refused, handing his friend the gun. After that, Morgan been moved to the press wing, writing news statements, leaflets – 'Provo promo' the people called it. To this day, he remembered the words of the training instructor in Donegal: 'with kneecaps, don't aim straight for the patella or you'll wreck the leg for life. Aim for the side of the knee to knock a bit of muscle back instead. But if it goes wrong, too bad. It's not like the fella's ever going to play for Liverpool, is it?'

He heated up some leftovers for his tea and sat down at his laptop. His plan was to read more about the vampire, but he couldn't concentrate. Through the open windows there was still a buzz in the street, some collective call reverberating. A smell of barbequed plastic and metal filtered into the air. It had already started. He walked back outside. The tricolour in the window opposite hung completely still. His neighbours were starting to head towards a wreath of smoke above the rooftops. He passed a couple of women who were sitting in deckchairs on the pavement, their glasses of wine perched on the window ledge, as if enjoying some open-air concert.

The sun was slowly disappearing like it was being lowered into a grave, while a fevered anticipation was rising. A teenage girl was running down the street, anarchically leaping up and slapping every 'to let' board in sight.

On the road next to the bonfire a car was burning. White police land rovers were screeching up to block the road and, behind Morgan, a squad of teenagers were coming out of dark entries in black skinny jeans and hoodies without brand names, scarves across their faces, gloves on their hands. They carried crates of petrol bombs and wheeled bins full of bricks. He could see Peadar Ó Mhichíl standing in the open, calling out instructions, gesticulating. He couldn't keep his eyes off him, taking in his fingernails on his right hand, kept long from playing the guitar. Long as a vampire's, thought Morgan. He kept looking at his hand and wondering – had Peadar's hand ever pulled a trigger? Had it set a bomb? Had it assembled, dissembled, or trembled? Had it beat a body, beat against bone? Had it lifted the earth with a spade? Had it robbed? Had it wiped away blood? Had it closed the eyes of a comrade? Had it written the words that could kill?

What did you do back in the day, Peadar, Morgan wanted to ask, but he already knew. The Provies in Derry hadn't done a tap, they'd been infiltrated, full of touts, full of sound and no action. You think you can make up for that, have another go at being a hero, Peadar, do you? Is this your last chance to make history on the backs of these boys? To ride on the coattails of anger over Brexit and the border? To feel the blood of the young pumping through your veins?

Morgan watched Peadar beckon over an MTV cameraman, and wondered if this whole show of strength tonight was for no other cause than Peadar's personal fame. A teenager in black walked past, a gun in his hand, and the strut and the slenderness reminded him of Seán Óg. He longed to run over and tackle him, but he'd never get away with it in this city. He was an outsider, and if your granny wasn't boxed and buried in the cemetery you'd always be an outsider. Suddenly, an image came into his vision of the teen who was kneecapped. The hit team had arrived at the teenager's country home, shot him, then cut the phone line so he couldn't call an ambulance, leaving him to bleed to death. Oh, god, the cruelty still rocked him. He could feel a stone pressing on his chest, crushing the breath out of him. The road quivered under his feet on a frequency he could no longer understand.

'Go back to your homes. Any trespassers on this road will be identified and arrested,' an officer was declaiming from his land rover's loud hailer. The tone was hysterical but the static buzz made his voice sound from a faraway moon.

Petrol bombs were being sparked up and hurled by the crowd. A land rover reversed down a side street in panic, its tyres alight, leaving trails of fire like a burning chariot. Next to Morgan, a female Sinn Féin councillor was yelling at some rioters who jabbed their fingers aggressively towards her face. She stepped back, powerless, retreating to her own clique. The journalists and camera operators were all standing on the police lines, jockeying for the best vantage point. Morgan thought he could see Jim, but in the strange haze of the steaming, burnt-out car the world was wavering. The bonfire had been struck by a petrol bomb and was turning into a pulsing red heart of heat that made him feel faint. The fireweed around it was catching light.

He watched the lithe figure of the gunman come out from behind a wall. The gunman pushed his chest forward like he wanted a bullet in it and fired three shots at the police. The crowd squealed and ducked as if the sky was falling in. There was a commotion up at the land rovers. Someone had been hit.

Morgan turned away. The smoke was percolating around him. He didn't want to be part of this war. He headed back up the road, past the pub with its long, empty bench outside, glittering with commemorative plaques. Although it was almost dark overhead there was still a thin parabola of lighter sky in the distance which he kept his eyes on. Soon, the quiet pad of feet overtook him, the teenagers fleeing back to their mothers', all swagger gone, murmuring in low, urgent voices that a young journalist called Ciara had been shot dead.

IRISH-AUSTRALIAN

We woke up to a cold morning in Portarlington, our host, Declan, crashing around in the kitchen to rouse us. I don't think he appreciated the fact we were musicians and were therefore up later than most, touring with a perma-hangover. A Belfast musician with a pint in the hand is as iconic a sight as a Belfast freedom fighter with a gun.

I padded into the kitchen just as Declan was disappearing out to the garden with a pair of secateurs. I checked my watch. 9am – and at eighty years of age he was out doing the gardening. These Irish-Australians were incorrigible. When he came back he had a cut rose in his hand. I watched him go over to the corner shelf and, below his wife's photo, replace a rose in a vase with a fresh one. He'd already told us she had died five years ago.

'That's beautiful,' I said, noticing how that portion of the room resembled a Marian shrine.

'A rose for my Gráinne every morning. I promised her before she died.' He turned and walked through to the hall. 'Now get up, you lazy bastards! It's breakfast time!' he shouted to the rest of the band. 'Craobh Rua, me arse,' he muttered. Craobh Rua was the name of our band, meaning Red Branch after the Celtic clan of warriors.

I cut a knife into the soft red skin of a tamarillo. I'd never tried one before, but it was delicious – like a tomato flavoured with the sweetness of mango.

Tina, Oisín and Maxi lumbered out of their rooms, yawning. Tina, wide-eyed, slightly-dazed, looked dubious about the tamarillos.

'Did you know,' she said, 'apparently you have to eat something thirty-two times to like it?'

Yesterday, we'd travelled on the train from Warrnambool to Geelong, shuttling past trees that had expired from the summer drought. The naked limbs of white-barked, leafless eucalyptuses lined the tracks. Maxi fell asleep against the window, leaving a little circle of condensation from his lips on the glass.

Typical of us, our travels didn't go to plan. We failed to get our instruments off the train at Geelong before the doors had closed and ended shuttling on for miles before catching a train back. Eventually, Declan picked us up in a people carrier, dustier than if it had been in the Dakar Rally. He drove us along the Great Ocean Road, lined with coastal trees, flat-topped from the wild Antarctic winds we'd felt whistle through us the past few days. We arrived in Portarlington at nightfall to the sight of huge white tents set up on the grass next to the seaside promenade. We were here for the National Celtic Festival and I could feel that surge of excitement in my belly at a new venue.

After breakfast the sun was hotting up, so I went for a walk into town. Declan's house was on the edge of the countryside, making for a tramp along the grassy verge. There was a spice in the air from the pepper trees. I passed a reedy pond, the bass notes of riveting frogs overlaid with the high pitch of crickets. As soon as I reached the pavements, magpies were fluting on every street corner. The festival site was full of workers in yellow neon jackets, hammering and drilling. Just beyond it were boats tethered in the blue, and I could see the skyscrapers of Melbourne hovering above the haze on the sea like a magical floating city.

At dusk Declan drove us down for the opening of the festival. There was a sunset of fevered pinks out on the bay. Oisín and Tina wanted to chill out on the pier drinking cans of beer and watching the sunset, but Maxi and I, being older, reckoned we should dander over to the 'Lighting of the Hearth' to please our funders. I was fifty one and a third. I don't know why I kept breaking my age down like that, but it must have been due to getting older and feeling I was running out of time. It was almost like when I was a child and every month seemed important.

We joined the crowd gathered round a trough full of burning wood. An Aboriginal guy in an anorak and a baseball cap, who was evidently the festival shaman, was waving a sheaf of smouldering grass in our faces, urging us to breathe in the smoke.

'Welcome in the good spirits!' he cried out. 'Cleanse yourselves!'

Tina pushed herself to the front and Maxi quipped 'don't give it to her. She's always smoking grass.' A few people tittered, but Tina ignored him, wafting the smoke towards her face.

'More,' she insisted, half invisible in its plumes.

'You must be planning to sin a lot tonight,' remarked the shaman, glittery-eyed.

I sucked some smoke in too and regretted it when my lungs rebelled and coughed it back up. A festival organiser handed me a lantern on a stick. It was covered in shamrocks and I felt like a tacky souvenir seller from back in Belfast. I trooped along with the other lantern-bearers to the Celtic Club, while Maxi, Tina and Oisín watched on in kinks, sniggering away at me. I suddenly realised I was being ushered onto the stage, but just in time I managed to palm my lantern off on some kid. We still had an hour to spare until our gig at eight, so we ate some soup in the green room, washed down with a few wines.

'Hey, Siobhán,' a man called out.

'Innes!' I shouted, hugging him. Innes was a Scottish guitarist I knew from years back.

'Ah, you remembered me.'

How could I forget anyone who said their name was the middle part of Guinness? He was in his early thirties now, tall, black-haired and with a sensitive pallor suggestive of a suffering artist that belied his party animal self. I fancied him, but what chance did I have apart from cryogenically freezing myself and waiting for him to age twenty years then kiss me awake like Snow White. As he was talking to me, I could see him glance across at Tina. Tina was twenty nine with big green eyes and lips as red as the inside of a Cherry Ripe.

'Craobh Rua, you're on!' called the backstage techie.

I picked up my fiddle and went out into the lights with Maxi, guitar, Tina, banjo and Oisín, pipes. I couldn't see the faces of the audience, but I heard the music of their murmurs as a prelude. We loved playing in tents because there was only a thin membrane between us and the stars; we felt we could almost lift the roof off.

It was a great gig and we ran off the stage buzzing. I got a pint in plastic and threaded my way outside. Maxi was there with an Australian friend of his, Joe. Joe was vaping heavily, exhaling white clouds.

'Are you smoking that or driving it?' joked Maxi.

'It's like gorillas in the mist,' I added.

'Am I a gorilla?' asked Joe, pretending to be offended.

I didn't think he was a gorilla at all. He was mid-fifties, silver-haired, blue-eyed and had a relaxed manner and a confident rise to his chin that might have been born from his lack of height, but was appealing. He told me his mother had been reared in Ireland and he was director of his own theatre company. He also revealed he was divorced and had a son who lived with him.

'I'm a great-uncle too. Well, great in that sense, but in the sense of being great as well,' he added lightly.

'I'm sure you are great,' I said.

Maxi came back with a tray of pints for us.

'Beautiful,' said Joe of the pint, but he was looking at me as he said it, and, even if it was a coincidence, I felt a spin in my heart.

We went back inside to watch the bands. I told Tina I wanted to be with Joe and she whooped 'yes!' breaking out into a huge grin. She advised me, however, not to fall too hard for him as we were leaving Portarlington the next day.

'You see, women fall for men harder than they fall for us,' she explained. 'It's because of our hormones.'

I'd never heard this theory before. 'Don't worry,' I assured her. 'I never fall too hard.'

'Perhaps it's because you're more masculine,' she shrugged.

Perhaps, but my hormones were all over the place with the menopause anyway, so who knew, though it was clear that Tina was still carrying the weight of her recent break-up.

'At least I'm getting over it. I'm starting to see the beauty in all that loss,' she said. 'Did you know, when you look at unhappy tears through a microscope, they have beautiful patterns like frost?'

Joe joined us. He started telling me about the time he went swimming and was circled by sharks. All Australians seemed to have these death-defying stories, whether it be with sharks, spiders or snakes, and we Irish couldn't get enough of them. My own most dangerous animal moment was being bitten by a Labrador at nursery school for sticking my finger in its ear, which didn't quite compete.

While we talked, a Celtic love ballad, 'Siúil a Rún', kept soaring through the tent, 'come, my love', again and again, urging me to speak out.

'Are you single?' I blurted out.

His eyes opened wider. 'Yes, I am.'

'Well, let's be single together then,' I said, making him laugh. 'Seriously though, I find you attractive.'

'I find you attractive too.'

'Great, then later we can spend time together.'

He nodded, smiling. 'Are you often this direct with men?' he wanted to know.

'No, I'm not. But I like you and I don't want to lose you.'

At midnight the Celtic Club closed and we all made our way out. Joe wanted to show me the stars of the Southern Cross but the sky was too misty. He was staying at the Grand Hotel, an old Victorian building rumoured to be full of ghosts. Most of the musicians were staying there too, as it had a fine bar and was party central for the festival. Maxi was already encamped at a table in the beer garden armed with a huge joint that was sputtering and sparking like an old motorbike.

'What are you smoking there, a didgeridoo?' Joe teased.

'Did you hear?' asked Oisín, bouncing over excitedly. 'There's an all-night party at a house with a purple door.'

'I'll pass, thanks.' I wasn't interested in one of Oisín's vague phantom parties. Back in Belfast, we once searched half the night for a party he told us was on Mellow Street. It turned out it was Melrose Street, two miles across town.

We bought schooners of Carlton and headed straight up to the sessions on the second floor. Innes was playing the guitar in some sort of hypnotic trance, oblivious to the fact Tina was sitting next to him. The one thing about musicians is they are too in love with music to ever care about love.

As Joe clutched his schooner, I noticed for the first time that the top part of his index finger was missing at the joint. I was curious but said nothing as I didn't want to make him self-conscious.

'One question,' Joe said. 'Do you like receiving?'

'Need you ask?' I laughed. He was talking my kind of language.

'I'm into tantric sex myself.'

'Brilliant.'

I told him about a song I'd recently composed about sex and its rejuvenating powers.

'You're absolutely right,' he agreed. 'Japanese geishas used to believe washing in sperm would keep them young.'

'I never knew that.'

There was nothing more to say, so I followed him along a corridor full of red doors. I could suddenly smell the shaman's smoke off my own skin, deep and acrid. Joe took out the key and unlocked it. It was a small box of a room, with an old-fashioned radiator, a sink topped with a miniature mirror, an ancient wardrobe, a red bedspread and matching curtains.

The second he closed the door, we began kissing and pulling our clothes off, almost collapsing onto the bed. He put his hands on my breasts and I caressed his arms, moving up his biceps onto his shoulders and back. He started licking my nipples till they stood out like bright redcurrants under the stark light above. Distracting shouts kept coming from the corridor, young Irish accents from wild room parties, the smash of a bottle. 'Whiskey in the Jar' was being piped out raucously from the beer garden below.

'Wait a second,' said Joe, jumping up to turn off the light. He opened the curtains and the outside lights from the beer garden gave off a subtle glow. The shouts seemed muffled now, almost subterranean, the music surreal, as we sank deeper in the rhythm of one another. Joe pushed me onto my back and nibbled my thighs and sucked, pulling gently inside me with his fingers as if pulling out the pulp from the skin of a fruit. We moved onto our knees and leant on each other, clasping our bodies in tightly while we touched. His hands worked on me delicately, making me feel like I was clay and he was creating me. I could feel the buzz, the core of white clitorial heat nerving through me.

While I sucked, he cradled his hand around my head. His cock went semi-hard, but not hard enough.

'Is it the drink?' I asked.

'Sort of,' he said, not wanting to break the quiet. He began to touch me again.

When I rolled away and lay beside him, the music outside had stopped.

'Tell me, what happened to your finger?'

'My brother bit it off.'

'What?'

'We were in a fight. It was just as well he bit it off or I would have killed him.'

'God ... family reunions must be a bit awkward, everyone looking at your finger.'

'No, he's been dead about five years now. He died of alcoholism. He was a real mess and we'd always had a difficult relationship.'

His voice was troubled and I regretted bringing it up.

'I better go.'

Joe switched on the light as I started putting on my clothes.

'Are you able to find your own way home?' he asked.

'Yeah, no problem. It's only fifteen minutes away.'

'Sorry, I'd go with you but I'm wrecked. I have a conference call at 9am.'

His face looked haggard in the light. I gave him a kiss goodbye.

'Come and see me before I leave in the morning,' he said.

'Ok. What time?'

'Any time. Let's say between ten and eleven?'

In a small place like Portarlington, there were no taxis at 1.30am. When I went downstairs the bar was closed up, a pale eerie night light illuminating the beer pumps. Outside, I began to walk along the main road, a few drunken shouts ringing out from others who'd left the sessions. I turned right, and then realised it was the wrong way. I pulled out my phone to check the route but there was no signal. For a second I wondered if I should go back to the Grand Hotel and stand outside to use their WiFi but instead I decided to press on. It was too cold to hang around.

The next turning seemed familiar with its flat-roofed colonial-style houses. After about a hundred yards, the pavements and street lights ebbed away and there was only the dark grass verge ahead. A car drove past and I was terrified the driver would stop as I was completely alone. I began to wish I'd gone back when I had the chance. The road in front seemed to curve into a white wall of mist. There was a small turn-off but I didn't recognise it. I couldn't tell if I'd passed the pond as the crickets had been quelled by the cold into silence.

My feet were soon soaking from the lush grass and the damp was creeping under my sleeves and collar. A set of car headlights were hurtling towards me like searching spotlights, and I jumped out of sight into the wet hedgerow. A dog barked from a garden, sensing me. Not one light was on in any of the houses, not even a porch light to make me think I could rouse the inhabitants if I was chased by some insane murderer. My heart was on hyperdrive, my ankles turning over on clumps of grass as I kept stumbling forward.

Finally, I stopped. The gardens were opening up into fields and the mist was passing in clouds. It was obvious I'd come way too far and I started heading back fast, trying to push my freezing limbs into action, wondering if I had the strength to keep walking for hours until daylight. It was ridiculous – it was hardly the outback, yet I'd wandered off into some survival movie of my own making. I was furious with myself.

Further on, I noticed the turn-off from before and realised as soon as I hit it that it was the right road. There was a gap in the hedge that emerged into a suburban cul-de-sac and, to my relief, I recognised the palm tree next to Declan's. I headed in through the gate and was even more thankful to find the front door open. In Victoria, they always leave the door open.

I woke up about nine and lay on, too drained to get up, too excited about seeing Joe again to fall back asleep. I finally had a shower at ten and soaped my muscles that still ached after sex and my impromptu nocturnal hike. I got dressed slowly, the aftereffects of the beer making the world seem a dreamscape. In the dining room I noticed a new red rose, a droplet teetering on its folds like a falling tear. I tried to catch the tear with my finger but the winter-petals were brittle and fell onto the dark wood.

'Hey, Siobhán, where are you off?' Declan asked as I opened the front door.

'Just going to see a friend.'

'You do bloody know I'm taking you all to Melbourne in an hour?'

'No worries,' I called back, closing the door on his testiness.

As I headed off down the cul-de-sac, I could hear the pond life fermenting and riffing and bubbling in its sun-heated stew. I felt a growing tingle; I couldn't wait to see Joe. I would only just make it there before eleven if I hurried. The festival was soon in front of me, and I could see straight into a stall full of Aran jumpers, shillelaghs and hippy hoodies adorned with mottos like 'Kiss me, I'm Irish'.

The bar was open at the Grand Hotel and I hurried through it, up onto the huge staircase. No 9 was his room. No 3, No 5, No 7 ... His door was wide open. Waiting for me, I thought.

The room was empty. The window was open, a breeze blowing back the red curtains. It was filled with light, evoking a different room, a different town, a different country even, from my memory. I wondered briefly if I'd misremembered the number, but no. The cleaners hadn't yet come and the white sheets from the night before were still there, creased from our heat.

I touched them lightly. I was the one who always left, who moved from place to place, but I had been so sure he was going to be there for me, it came as a shock. Hadn't he wanted to touch me again? I stood there, feeling the ghost of him, feeling a loneliness I hadn't experienced in some time, before I went over to the window and looked out.

Melbourne, floating in the haze, was waiting for me.

THE CURE FOR TOO MUCH LOVING

Bronagh first met him while she was out with her old school friends in the Northern Whig. It was only a few weeks after breaking up with Matt, her boyfriend of five years. She'd run back to Belfast to lick her wounds and hadn't been meaning to meet anyone new until she saw this man lounging against the bar, his green eyes gunned on her, a curl on his lips like he was on the verge of saying something clever. His suede jacket was black and it was funny how the tassels hanging from the sleeves matched the tassels on her handbag.

Her friends, Anna and Erin, were cadging drinks off a couple of country boys in return for some playful flirting. Although the man was chatting to the barman, his eyes kept moving back to hers in a perfect synchronicity. He made her nervous because his black hair was shaved and his fist was resting on the bar as if steeled for a fight, yet his shirt was buttoned right up to his throat like he was dressed for a formal, and it made her curious.

'Hello,' he said, coming over with a grin. His name was Ciaran, and at twenty seven he was four years older than her.

'What do you do?' she asked.

'What I like.'

'I'm unemployed myself,' she confessed, telling him she'd recently left her sub-editing job in England. She didn't mention Matt. 'Just moved back in with my parents,' she added, a bit embarrassed.

Anna and Erin were moving on to another bar, so she asked him to put his number into her phone. When his hand brushed against hers, it felt rough and full of skelfs. Once she was outside, she glanced back through the huge windows. They were steamed up, but drips of condensation were running down it like teardrops. Through the drips, she noticed he was still looking out at her.

At home, she was crying a lot about Matt. It was the grief of losing him, together with anger at how he'd thrown her out of their rented house in Gillingham. The sorrow came over her at all sorts of random, unsuitable moments in the day; when she was watching TV with her parents; in the queue at Tesco's checkout. Matt had confronted her because she'd been seen kissing another guy at a party. It was true she'd slept with this guy, but it was the only occasion in five years she'd cheated on Matt, and it had occurred in a drunken haze. At the time, she'd only had brief flashes of the guy on top of her and couldn't even remember his scent or the taste of his kisses – it was like it never happened. Of course, she should never have done it, but it was hard to think of such a vague encounter as a betrayal.

Later that week she plucked up the courage to call Ciaran. She went into town to meet him on one of those

November evenings where the sky was electric orange; it looked like lava was flowing into the grey ashes of cloud. In High Street, the office windows shone like fragments of burning sun were stored within.

She already had misgivings about meeting Ciaran because, in a stroke of bad timing, Matt had been in touch by text that very morning. He'd said he couldn't face the thought of a future without her, and asked her to fly over to talk things through. She'd thought about it long and hard, but she still loved him, so she answered back 'yes.'

Ciaran was waiting for her in the Northern Whig. It was as though he hadn't moved an inch from the night they'd met.

She ordered a gin and tonic.

'And a peach cider for me,' he told the barman.

'Peach cider,' she teased.

'What would you prefer? A pint of Guinness? Is that butch enough for you?' he laughed and explained, 'I used to dream of sweet cider in Maghaberry.'

'You were in prison? What for?'

'Giving date rape drugs to girls,' he joked, before seeing her eyes widen. 'Sorry, only kidding!'

He told her all about it. How some years ago he'd been in Óglaigh na hÉireann when the peelers had raided his house and uncovered information on his laptop.

'You do know I'm a Prod,' she said, uncomfortably.

'Oh, I know. Christ, I'm really putting my foot in, aren't I? The date rape joke, telling you I was once a mad-dog republican – at this rate you'll never want to see me again!'

'Maybe you'll never want to see me again,' she countered, and admitted she was going to Gillingham to see her ex.

'Ah. So this is it then.'

'Yeah, but I'm not sure Matt and I will work things out.'

'Ah, I know how these things go. The moment you see him you'll be back with him.'

She was quiet, wondering. She already dreaded seeing the hurt again in Matt's eyes. The night they'd broken up, she'd seen the fury in him and he'd tortured her till dawn with the one unanswerable why. He'd always been so kind to her but she didn't trust that anymore. And how could she go back with him when a few months down the line he might resort to some sort of revenge fuck just to pay her back?

'So – a Norwegian?' asked Ciaran.

'A what?'

'Anorr' wee gin, as we say here,' Ciaran joked, and she was grateful to him for keeping things light.

After one more drink they left. He insisted on walking her home, even though the Cregagh Road was a brave step away. He lived in North Belfast himself.

As they strolled towards the east, they linked arms. He told her he was a bodhrán maker, and he used the softest goat skins which were reserved for Lambeg drums, so, never minding his republican past, he was good friends now with the Orangemen. The wood he got was from the graveyards and parks, but sometimes he even poached wood himself from ashes, mulberries and oaks in the countryside. His granda knew the land, he said, as he'd been an Irish traveller.

They walked down the narrow, shuttered Woodstock Road, past the electric white of the chip shops. She noticed that the library windows had cracks in the glass fanning out like huge spiders' webs, and his words gave her a yearning for country lanes and hedgerows.

The Woodstock soon morphed into the Cregagh and the road grew wider, surrounded by suburban gardens. Outside her house they stopped, faced each other and he took her hands, drawing them round his waist, 'to warm them,' he said. A slab of streetlight fell across his cheekbone. She leaned back against the hedge; it felt soft as a bed and she imagined the world tilt so she'd be lying down with him. She couldn't invite him in as her parents were old-fashioned and, even worse, light sleepers. Once when she was sixteen, she'd brought a boy into the porch for a kiss, and her mother had shouted down, thinking they were burglars.

'I really hope I see you again,' she said.

'I'll still be here if it doesn't work out in England.' He gave her a kiss on the lips and left. Her lips were so cold she hardly felt it.

That night she dreamt of bombs, exploding laptops and sweet scents. Someone had told her that bombs in the Troubles had smelt of marzipan. It had always struck her as strange as she loved the taste of marzipan.

Over the next few days there was no contact from Matt. It wasn't until two weeks later that he texted her out of the blue to apologise. He'd upgraded his phone and some messages had been withheld, including hers. She wanted to tell him she couldn't stand the thought of never being in his warmth again, but her fingers hovered and stalled above the keys. Surely he should have phoned to talk things through, rather than coldly texting, like he was arranging a night out instead of their whole future together.

'It was a pity I didn't get to see you,' she texted.

He didn't respond. She understood he'd already mentally parted from her.

She immersed herself in job interviews with recruitment agencies. She went out with her girlfriends and made contact with other old school pals, excited about being back. It crossed her mind to contact Ciaran again but there was a fatalism about things now. The timing of meeting

Ciaran when she hadn't fully pulled away from Matt meant it wasn't to be.

A few weeks later, she ended up in the Northern Whig with Anna and Erin. She glanced at the bar. A few guys were leaning against it, but seemed more interested in their own reflections in the bar mirrors than the girls around them.

At about one o'clock her friends booked a taxi, but Bronagh decided to walk home on her own. She was just heading down Pottinger's Entry when she saw him coming towards her, his head hunched forward, his fists thrust in his pockets.

'Ciaran!'

He didn't seem surprised; a big smile shaped itself on his lips. He'd been hanging out with the bodhrán players in the Garrick.

'I'll walk you home,' he said, locking arms with her.

Over the next month, they went out together every Friday and Saturday. He always walked her home and they exchanged no more than a brief kiss on the lips. All the men she'd ever known had fumbled and groped – any normal man surely would have made a physical move on her by now. In the early days Matt had been a one-man orgy, but Ciaran reminded her of old country courtships she'd only read about. Even so, she felt the tautness in his body at the hedge. One time when he held her by the waist he said with a laugh 'you're wearing more skins than a nun,' and she thought he was about to pull her layers up to touch her, but his hands stayed where they were. She wanted to grab him tight, but it was a dance neither wanted to take the lead in. She guessed he was so good-looking he always waited for the girls to throw themselves on him, though perhaps all he wanted was to walk and talk. It was mad as the less he touched her the more she wanted him. She wondered why he didn't invite her back to his house, but something made her hesitant to ask.

Her parents, she knew, wouldn't approve of him. The way he walked quickly with his bunched fists, close into the hedge, not wanting to be seen. A republican too. They'd loved Matt, the man who'd hurt her the most, and it felt good to be out standing on the road these nights with Ciaran without them knowing a thing of it. Just by the hedge where they stood there was a pink flower that kept surviving the winter frosts and gales. Every day she thought it would be gone, but every day it clung on to life.

She and Ciaran were having a late night drink in the Northern Whig when she finally felt drunk enough to say 'why do we never do anything, you and me?'

'I've been thinking about it myself,' he said, biting his lip. 'Look. I'm not going to see you anymore.'

She was floored. 'Why not?'

'You're just too pure for me. It's better I just leave you to your nice life on the Cregagh Road. With your friends.'

'But I don't want all that ... I want you ...'

The tears rose in her and she was shocked at herself. It was as if she couldn't take rejection so soon after Matt.

'Don't cry,' he said. 'People are looking. Jesus, they'll think I've beaten you up or something!' he added, trying to make her smile.

He led her out of the bar. 'Come on.'

They went to a quiet part of Pottinger's Entry while people passed by, their shoes cracking on the cobbles.

'I live with a girl,' he explained. 'That's why I've never brought you back. I've lived with her for three years and I've told her about you. The only way this can work is if it's us three together, and I know you won't want that.'

'Oh,' said Bronagh, letting it sink in.

'It's alright. I'll let you go back to your quiet life. You need a conventional boyfriend, someone to look after you.'

'Don't judge me, Ciaran,' she snapped back at him. The last thing she wanted was a boring, preordained future, and Ciaran surely knew that. By letting her go, it was like he was daring her, trying to manipulate her.

'It's fine,' he said softly, and she wondered if he was genuinely giving her the chance to leave. 'I'll walk you home.'

She arranged to meet Ciaran and Leah in Cassidy's on the Antrim Road, as it wasn't far from their house. It was just to meet up, Ciaran said, and see what would happen. After months of repressed kisses she so longed for Ciaran's body she was happy to agree to anything. But when she thought about Leah, all she had was an image of white, soft skin – she stopped herself from imagining more. The only sexual fantasies Bronagh had ever had were about men. On the rare occasions she'd had a sexual dream about a woman she'd woken up disturbed, trying to escape from it. Oh, of course, she'd had a couple of regulation teenage crushes on other girls, but she'd more craved glances from them than kisses, approval rather than sex.

Luckily, she didn't have much time on her hands to stress about it as she was starting a temping job as a receptionist at a brewery. It wasn't until lying in bed the night before meeting Leah that she grew afraid she'd be repelled by another woman's body. She was on the brink of texting Ciaran to cancel when she noticed, in the bright orange light from the blinds, her body stretching out straight in front of her, her toes tipped upwards, and imagined herself laid out in a coffin, sliding into the flames of a crematorium, and the fear that she was too scared to even live gripped her. The same thought kept swirling round her mind, urging her not to back out; why else had she been released from a life of safety with Matt but to experience something different?

By the time Bronagh arrived at Cassidy's, Leah and Ciaran were already sitting in a snug. Leah was small, curvy, pretty and had dyed blonde hair. It was a relief that Leah looked different as it felt they weren't in competition.

Ciaran started telling Bronagh all about how he'd met Leah when she'd been living with another guy in Magherafelt. He'd asked her to leave the guy, but she'd refused.

'Then, one night when he was away, you came round and you wouldn't take no for an answer. You loaded up all my things in your car,' Leah said, looking at him with a smile. 'It was like you were rescuing me!'

'You needed rescue from that loser,' Ciaran said, trying to play the romance down in front of Bronagh. 'The guy was so bad at sex he used KY jelly!'

But his eyes were fixed on Leah, making Bronagh feel like an eavesdropper. She wondered if she'd made a terrible mistake in coming, but Leah was friendly towards her and seemed genuinely chilled out.

'So, where did you two meet?' Leah asked.

She directed her question at Bronagh, but Ciaran jumped in tensely.

'Oh, just in town.'

'He never remembers a thing,' smiled Leah. 'Do you remember, Bronagh?'

'Oh, well,' said Bronagh, trying not to give too much away. 'It was just one night in the Northern Whig.'

Leah looked at him suspiciously. 'But you told me you never go into the Northern Whig.'

'Well, I must have gone one night,' said Ciaran firmly. 'Am I not allowed?'

'No, you are,' granted Leah, squeezing out another smile.

Bronagh changed the subject and began to chat to them about her new job in a brewery. Nearby, the traditional session started up, buoyant, quick and fun.

'I might have known you'd end up with a job related to your drinking hobby,' joked Ciaran, happy to keep things flirty and light.

Ciaran suggested going home at about eleven. They'd only had three drinks apiece, and Bronagh felt relaxed but clear-headed. She wouldn't have exactly said she was attracted to Leah, but, as she rationalised to herself, she found her attractive. Outside, stars were pulsing in the sky and she thought back to her old childhood belief that if the stars shone at night the next day would be perfect.

Ciaran and Leah lived in a ramshackle three-storey house. The house had been in Ciaran's family for years. There were so many weeds sprouting from the roof, thought Bronagh, it looked like a rooftop garden. Two terriers scuffed noisily around their feet as they came through the front door.

They went straight up to the bedroom. As they took off their clothes, Ciaran kept chatting lightly. It was freezing, Bronagh noticed, though she was sure she was quivering from nervousness too. Apparently, there was an old aga in the kitchen, but it was the only heating they had.

The three of them got into bed, Ciaran in the middle. Bronagh wrapped her arm round his chest. Her forearm brushed lightly against Leah's and automatically she pulled it away. Ciaran turned to Leah and started kissing her. Under the covers Bronagh traced her fingers down his body, but he took hold of her hand and led it over to Leah.

So, it happens just like that, thought Bronagh later, as she felt Ciaran inside her, then Leah licking her, the three bodies squeezing and squirming in between each other lithely, chaotically, twisting and twitching. She could smell candles strongly in the high-ceilinged room, but the only light came from the bedside lamps.

The strange thing was that she felt her fingers drawn to Leah's inner folds as naturally as she would have touched herself. Leah's skin was as soft as she'd imagined, but her touch was as hard as a man's.

When they were lying exhausted, still throbbing from each other's bodies, Leah asked her 'did you smell the candles?'

'It's the ghosts,' Ciaran explained. 'Sometimes at night you can smell the candles they used to light in here.'

'Wow,' said Bronagh, still sex-dazed.

When Ciaran went to the toilet, Leah said to her 'I've never fancied women before, have you?'

'No,' Bronagh said, sharing in the revelation. 'Never.' But it occurred to her that maybe it wasn't true.

'Come on, Bronagh,' said Ciaran, rubbing his arms from the cold as he came back in and picked up his jeans. 'I'll walk you home.'

Over the next month, the three met once a week in different bars and went home together. Afterwards, Ciaran would always walk her back to her parents' house. At that hour in the morning the streets were eerie, but it was their private time together, away from Leah. Ciaran revealed to her that he'd had threesomes when he'd lived with another girl.

'I've probably ruined you now for all future men!' he laughed. 'You'll find the sex too boring.'

He now kissed her freely. His angular unshaven face felt like a rough-hewn stone. One night when there was a full moon haloed with a rainbow, he invited her to his house on a Sunday afternoon when Leah would be out.

Bronagh came round that Sunday to find him shambling about in his work clothes – an old pair of combats and a wool jumper flecked with wood shavings. He showed her his workshop at the back of the house, the lathes, the many goat skins on the table. He picked up a newly-made bodhrán.

'Look,' he urged. He pulled her hand over to touch a divot in the smooth ash. 'Know what that's from?'

She shook her head.

'A bullet. From the Troubles. It was lodged in a tree near the Europa. I had my eye on that tree for years and finally the council cut it down and I claimed it.'

He drummed his fingers lightly on the skin.

'See?' he said, entranced. 'You can hear the history, the pain of the Troubles in the wood. It makes it even more beautiful.'

She watched him drum on, lost in his own rhythm. An image flashed through her head of his fingers playing with Leah.

Upstairs, he held her vice-like by the hips as she crashed down on his chest, the silver chain round her neck swinging into her mouth like a pair of reins.

Afterwards, she asked 'do you think Leah will ever leave you?'

'No way. She once told me she was lucky to have me. She still feels lucky. That's how I know she'll never leave.'

Bronagh came to the house every Sunday from then on. It was more intense when she and Ciaran were alone, and more fun when it was the three of them.

'That's one orgasm for me, two for Ciaran, and nil for Bronagh,' joked Leah one night.

'Right, Bronagh, your turn to score,' laughed Ciaran, pressing his lips to her skin.

Another night he complained that all the sexual attention was turned on him.

'Right, we better get ready for some hot lesbo sex,' Leah grinned, reaching for Bronagh.

Later, when Ciaran left the room, Leah said, a bit troubled, 'I suppose all this makes us lesbians now.'

'No, it doesn't. A bit bisexual at the most.'

'I'm not even sure,' said Leah. 'Surely you have to sleep with a woman on her own to be bisexual.'

'You're right,' agreed Bronagh. 'We need a new term for you and me. What about heteroflexual?' and they both laughed.

But it was strange to think she'd wound up having sex with a woman out of love for a man. The notion unsettled her.

The start of spring came, still cold but the nights were brighter and the tips of the branches bulged red, pregnant with leaves. Bronagh's job in the brewery was nearly at an end, but she already had a teaching course lined up for September over in England.

One Friday night she went into town to meet Ciaran and Leah. The sky was orange-tinged and chimneys coughed out purple smoke that gradually drifted into pink.

As soon as she stepped into the Northern Whig, Anna and Erin shouted out to her. She hadn't seen them since Christmas and, although Ciaran and Leah were at the bar, she headed straight for her friends.

'Long time, no see,' Anna said. 'Your boy's over at the bar, I notice.'

'With another girl,' said Erin accusingly. 'Look at them together.'

'That's Leah. She's just a friend of his,' Bronagh said unconvincingly, but it was clear Ciaran and Leah were a couple. Leah was sitting on a bar stool while he leant against the bar and the two were so close they were touching. It appeared almost as if he was guarding her.

After a quick catchup with her friends, Bronagh went to the bar.

'Hey,' she said, but Ciaran and Leah's response was muted. 'Sorry my friends are here tonight.'

'Fine,' Ciaran said with a cool shrug. 'You do what you have to. We'll be here for a while.'

She looked round at Anna and Erin, feeling their eyes burn into her. It shouldn't have mattered but, for some reason, she was wildly self-conscious and felt she should go back to them.

'I don't know how you can stick him being with another girl,' grumbled Anna, offended on Bronagh's behalf. 'Flaunting her right in your face. It's time you told him to fuck off.'

'I know,' said Bronagh, ashamed. Her friends, of course, had no inkling she was with Leah too, but she couldn't help thinking it was crazy to take part-share of a man. Maybe Matt leaving her had crushed her so much she no longer felt worthy of having her own man.

She glanced over unhappily at Ciaran and Leah. They didn't give anything away, but they weren't talking much to each other. They seemed to be awaiting her return. Viewing them through the prism of Anna and Erin, she felt an unexpected surge of jealousy.

'Hoof this down and forget about him,' urged Erin, handing her a shot glass.

She skulled the Jägermeister and turned her back to the bar, joining in flirting with some young students they'd met. After a few more shots, when she eventually looked round again, Ciaran and Leah had left.

She was suddenly distraught. What did Erin and Anna know about sex and love? All she could taste on her tongue was salt and blood. She made her excuses to the girls that she wasn't in the form for an all-nighter and they gave her sympathetic hugs and let her go, assuming she was heading home to mourn the loss of Ciaran. Once out in the street she started walking fast towards the Antrim Road. She was aching to be with Ciaran, and with Leah too – it was as if Leah was part of his body now.

Their house lay in darkness. They'd already gone to bed. She looked up at their window imagining their bodies twined without her. She quickly rapped on the front door. One of the terriers gave a warning bark but no light came on upstairs. She picked up some gravel from under a hedge and started throwing it up at the window. She didn't even care if they yelled at her and told her to fuck off. She just needed them to know she wanted them. A few seconds later the window pulled up and Ciaran leant out, bare-torsoed.

'I'll come down,' he called. 'It's Bronagh,' she could hear him telling Leah.

He opened the front door, naked in the dark shadows.

'I didn't think you were coming,' he said. 'We were nearly asleep there.'

He stepped past her onto the threshold a second, looking up at the house on the other side of the road. A woman was peeking down at them from the second-floor window and he mischievously pushed his hips out at her.

'It's the doctor's wife,' he explained with a laugh as he retreated indoors. 'Just giving her a quick thrill.'

Bronagh followed him up to the bedroom and got undressed, slipping into their bed. Leah didn't say a word, but Ciaran kept up his usual light chatter.

'Let me guess,' Ciaran grinned. 'It didn't even cross your friends' minds that we three could be together, did it?'

'No.'

She felt Leah's coldness, and it made her feel cold and sullen herself.

Ciaran started touching Bronagh, but Leah lay behind him, looking up at the ceiling, motionless. There was nothing in her face but a stoic passivity, delicate and pale. Bronagh could hardly bring herself to respond to Ciaran, and she couldn't understand if it was out of anger or sympathy for Leah. For the first time she was a total interloper in their life, a gatecrasher in their bed.

'Right,' said Ciaran, irritated. 'This isn't happening tonight. I don't know what's wrong with you both. I'll walk you home, Bronagh.'

They pulled on their clothes quickly. As they left the room, Leah was still staring up at the ceiling like she wanted to burst through it.

Outside, there was a raw feel to the air. Rain was on its way. The ring of Ciaran's boots on the pavement sounded strangely hollow.

They walked past the Catholic Church with its icon of Jesus on the cross.

'When I was a kid, I saw that statue and said to my Mum "who's that girly-looking boy"?' laughed Ciaran.

He kept talking about his childhood memories as they walked, reflecting that he'd always known he'd be different to other people; he'd recognised that uniqueness in Bronagh too from the outset. But Bronagh couldn't take his words in. The image of Matt slipped back into her mind and she expected to feel some pang, but there was nothing there anymore and she was glad of it.

At her hedge Ciaran kissed her goodnight. He didn't ask her to call him that week.

She stopped before she reached the front door and looked round at the moon. In four months' time she'd be back in England again. Light cloud was beginning to caul the sky from the west, but, through it, the stars were still glimmering.

THE LOTTERY OF STRANGERS

Folk in the west of Ireland believe that if you tell a story to someone you lose a little piece of your soul. Well, that's according to my ex-housemate, John Paul from Donegal, but I'm prepared to tell the story and take the risk. It's really a tale of two houses within a rented house in Belfast, a tale of two men diametrically opposed in culture and levels of hygiene.

You couldn't help liking John Paul. He was yawningly pale, fidgety, with a complexion like porous soda bread, and in spite of his thinness he had the constitution of a man who'd gone straight from the breast to Guinness. He worked hard as a barman, but in the house he was always slothful; you'd find him in the living room, grinning at Ulster TV, his arms stretched out over the sofa, his legs flying around trying to find a comfortable nesting place to roost.

John Paul was a typical Irishman as he had the words for about forty shades of rain; he could even tell between wet rain and damp rain. He had the charming bonhomie of a drinker – 'tilt your arm a bit further there,' he'd urge and, taking the cue from Gianni's civilised drinking habits, he'd begin extolling the virtue of a daily glass of wine for your health, the difference being he'd stretch it to a few glasses to make up for all those years it had been missing from his diet. This leads us on to the antisocial side of him. He had a tendency to flake out on the sofa after a skinful, and we had an inkling that the damp patches the following morning might have emanated more from poor bladder control than spilt alcohol.

John Paul's general slovenliness was anathema to Gianni who came from Italy. He fancied himself as an Italian stallion, but at five foot six he was more a little pony. Alternately saturnine and light-hearted, he tended to dominate the household with whatever mood he was in. I was the only housemate laid-back enough to have survived more than six months with him; he doused the house liberally in bleach, hoping to exorcise the wandering remains of former housemates. It was a bit much because wherever I set my towel down in the bathroom it picked up bleach stains. He worked as a pizza chef and made a lot of dough from making dough. He lived in the front room with his shy, pretty girlfriend, who matched his paranoia with her own hyper nervousness.

Two weeks ago I came home after work to find a detective sitting in our living room. I wasn't thrilled as the police always bring me out in a cold sweat and I start wondering if they're still after me for refusing to move from the road in last year's anti-capitalist protests. To me their mere existence could qualify as harassment. In any case, I'm always sure democracy is only one step from the gulag.

With all those scenarios in my head I was almost relieved to know we'd had a burglary. Eilis, Gianni's girlfriend, had managed to disturb the burglars, but they'd still had time to go through our rooms and I'd had fifty quid cash stolen.

Eilis was giving a statement, looking very shaken, her

hands wrapped round her knees. She was halfway through when Gianni burst in like a whirlwind.

'It was no burglar. Someone from in here done this,' he insisted dictatorially to the detective. 'Fingerprint everyone in the house.'

I stifled a laugh and the detective let slip a tiny smile, flaring her eyes at me, which I returned. 'Welcome to the madhouse,' I wanted to tell her.

'You think somebody you know's done this?' she checked with me.

I diplomatically mentioned that we'd had quite a procession of housemates who'd scarpered very suddenly, often with the keys. I omitted to say they'd usually been driven to it by Gianni, the one-man mafia.

'Where is John Paul tonight?' Gianni wanted to know, a strange look on his face.

'No, Gianni,' said Eilis, guessing what he was hinting at. 'The burglars have trashed his room too.'

If anything I thought it looked like the burglars had tidied it.

The police said that the burglars had chiselled through the kitchen window, but Gianni refused to believe it.

'Professional, my arse,' he grumbled. 'Experts know nothing. You never see the doctor who leave the scissors in the stomach and sew it back up?'

For the next couple of days Gianni skulked around our backyard looking for signs of entry and kept giving me a heart attack, his face popping up at the kitchen window like an evil fairy.

He was convinced that the burglar, whoever it was, had used a front door key. 'You understand the way?' he asked me. 'Too many people looking at me when I doing well, when I have nice stuff. Next time, I touch my balls for luck. Hey, fuck you all, you who looking at me!'

I didn't remotely believe it was any of our ex-housemates, although it did baffle me why on their way out they felt they had to steal something from us like it was a souvenir from a foreign country. Even the low-watt light bulbs would go, not to mention the cutlery that was so bent it looked like it had passed through the hands of Uri Geller. But I always loved when Gianni talked of the old times. Whatever you may say about us, Gianni and me, we have seen off the weirdos – not to mention the snails we shared our hall with for a few days. Ah, yes, and we also put flight to the landlord during the Great Rent Revolt of 2018.

However, more sinisterly, it soon became clear he'd taken it into his head that John Paul was in some way responsible for the burglary.

'Look,' he said, calling me out into the hall and showing me the scratches on his Vespa made by John Paul when he'd fallen down the stairs. 'Look what the dickhead done.'

'It's not that bad,' I replied. 'You can barely see it.'

Gianni and Eilis both eyed me with hostility. They'd been hoping to merge with me in a takeover bid of the house in order to oust John Paul. To be honest, I'd had enough of their machinations and felt it was high time I opted out of their Axis of Evil. I didn't object to living with John Paul, and I was tired of new housemates every month.

On my way through to the kitchen, John Paul was standing wobbling like a scarecrow in the wind, helping himself to another can. There was never a mark on him from his entanglements with the Vespa. It didn't surprise me as I imagined his rubbery physique would always come off better in a one to one struggle. Even when you'd just be standing there minding your own business, he'd accidentally stab you with a cigarette, being utterly unimpeded by the central commands of his nervous system.

'Did Il Duce mention me?' he asked, and he shrugged when I didn't answer. 'It's all right, better to say nothing. When I've been wronged I don't say a word. I leave it and sometimes it takes days or sometimes it takes five years for the wheel to turn but, sure enough, it does. And sometimes I'm after seeing what's happened and I go to god, "Now why did you do that? That was a wee bit more cruel than I'd have been." Oh, it'd surprise you how cruel god can be.'

If anyone had the right to know, it was John Paul, himself a statistic of divinely-inspired demographics. He'd been christened John Paul as his conception had coincided with a Papal visit to Ireland and the ensuing parental renunciation of condoms. Gianni was pretty well tuned into god's mysterious ways himself; whenever he had a headache you'd see him crossing himself with a finger dipped in olive oil. Anyway, as I'd stepped out of the equation I was very interested to see where god would stand on all this.

John Paul stayed well away from Gianni over the next few days. He buried his head deep in *The Kama Sutra* which he said was a fascinating book, although he suspected the only way it would help him to get girls would be by hitting them on the head with it. I thought he was being unduly modest. After all, after a few pints he was more flexible than anyone I'd ever met.

When I arrived home on a Wednesday night all the lights of the house were on, and the books and magazines in the living room were upturned on the floor. For one horrible moment I thought it was another burglary until I saw Gianni in the kitchen rifling through the bin bag in a frenzy.

'I losta my ticket,' Gianni wailed at me. 'I no joking. It gone away, disappear.'

He was so upset, it took me a while to understand. It

transpired the numbers he used each week on the lottery had just come up, netting him one point two million. The major bummer was he'd misplaced the ticket.

'Don't worry, we'll find it together,' I promised him, stifling an impulse to negotiate a preliminary cut in the million for myself.

Eilis, John Paul and I joined him in the search – fortunately John Paul proved willing to put his hand down the back of the sofa. At midnight we gave up and went to bed, but I could still hear Gianni feverishly pacing downstairs. I really felt for the man and prayed he would find it for his sake. I then got to thinking how I could move into his and Eilis's room which was far bigger than mine. He'd probably leave the six-pack of bleach behind too. It was an all-win situation.

The following day when I came back from work, I noticed a few dodgy-looking individuals scouring our street. Someone was even using their foot to turn over the dock leaves and dandelions proliferating outside our front door and I wondered how the word had spread. Then Gianni emerged from the hall accompanied by a TV crew. He had gone public with his story. He was upbeat, optimistic, clad in new Milanese tailoring that he'd just paid a fortune for.

'Believe me what,' he breezed to me and John Paul. 'Ever you taste rice with champagne? When I find my ticket I'll let you taste.'

John Paul fired me a look over his *Kama Sutra* and whispered 'the shop where he got his ticket definitely sold the winning numbers. Problem is, he can't prove he was there as the shop camera had run out of tape. Now all the oul loony bins are crawling out of the woodwork with the same story.'

Later, we switched on the news and watched Gianni make a promise to split the money with whoever found the ticket, but I felt slightly embarrassed when the interviewer waved a hand round our living room, using the words 'escape from rented squalor'. On the bookshelf behind her you could just make out the copy of *The Kama Sutra* snuggling up to *Hitler and Eva Braun: A Love Affair*. Eilis hovered into the camera's sights now and then, her dark, worried eyes out on stalks, her crumpled pink cardigan on her curved back, making her look like a frail prawn floating about in the murky depths of our living room.

When CNN phoned Gianni's mobile at eight o'clock the next morning I realised just how much Gianni, the telegenic pizza maker with the amusing grammar, had caught hold of the public's imagination. He was threatening to go global until the terrible news came – at noon it was announced that the one point two million had been claimed.

Gianni was inconsolable. At one o'clock I answered the door, hoping it was maybe one of his Italian friends armed with a sedative. It was the police. Again I broke out in a sweat, sure they were onto me. Wasn't it the same detective who'd asked me at the demo if I was determined to be arrested?

I guessed it wasn't every day that the police got a call to investigate the theft of a million. I imagined their little hearts had initially skipped a beat at the exciting prospect of maybe for once being asked to crack a heist, but they said there was nothing they could do about a case like this. A consortium of local refuse collectors had come forward with the winning ticket, claiming it had belonged to them all along.

'It's no possible, you understand? I always left it here, so someone he steal it,' said Gianni, pointing to the table beside the sofa, narrowing his eyes at John Paul.

I wondered if it was possible ... no, it wasn't worthy of me to think it. All the same, he definitely held something against Gianni ... could John Paul have stashed the ticket, then given it to the binmen? He could have struck a deal with them. No, I was being crazy! It was mad. Living with a succession of strangers was turning me as paranoid as Gianni.

Later that night, John Paul was drunk downstairs, and I could hear him stagger into the wet yard. From the kitchen I could see him tilt his chin up towards the sky and point a cigarette accusingly into the air.

'If you don't mind me saying, that was awful cruel of you. Altogether terrible. I would never have gone that far myself,' I heard him slur into the heavens as a rain that didn't know to stop fell steadily.

FUTURE-PROOF YOUR LIFE (STEP 7 OF 10)

So, it was the night I was about to do my TEDx talk at Stormont with ten other women. I'd been practising for days, but was still ropey with my lines. The ridiculous thing was I shouldn't even have been doing this talk – I'd drunk too much at a garden party a few months back and blagged my way onto the lineup. I had a history of overindulging in free wine and misrepresenting myself as an expert in various fields. I once passed myself off as a photographer at a gallery and agreed to furnish material for a solo exhibition. I didn't so much as own a camera for Christ's sake! I wasn't even part of generation selfie. I don't know why I felt I had to lie – I guess somewhere deep inside me there was a frustrated exhibitionist.

I arrived at Stormont at dusk. I was feeling well-groomed and fortunately it had stayed dry, as on drizzly days my hair went as bushy as Aberdeen Angus. I got out of the taxi and surveyed the twinkling lights over the south of the city – you could feel like a mini-god with that vista stretching out before you.

The other speakers were congregating in the green room and my god complex immediately retreated. They were all looking glamorous. Apart from one girl who was speaking about the gay community, I was the only one dressed in jeans. I didn't like dresses because I couldn't bear the spinal and orthopaedic torture contraption that were the accompanying high heels, and I didn't see why I had to wear heels anyway – at five foot ten compared to most Belfast men I was virtually a circus act on stilts.

All the speakers had big profiles and all-encompassing smiles to match. I had a low-key job in community arts, but I'd also written a few articles in local papers which helped. The biggest star of the night, Ana Matronic, was the last to arrive. She was smooth, beaming, metallic-dressed, exuding the steely charisma of an intergalactic star. She had such a patina of confidence even her skin looked airbrushed.

A young guy was bringing us in tea, coffee, sandwiches and platters of fruit.

'Where's the alcohol?' I asked.

'Later,' he grinned. He had an American accent. 'We don't want you rolling off the stage.'

'It's not for me.' I indicated Ana Matronic. 'We have a rock star here, and there's no booze? She's gonna freak! You'll probably get a guitar bust over your head!'

Luckily, I was speaker no. 4 and wasn't going to have to wait too long. The three speakers scheduled before me were manically rehearsing their lines, so I went out to the deserted corridor for a run-through, but kept stalling. With me, practice does not make perfect. Practice makes nervous. I'm honestly one of those types who is better off ingesting loads of drink and drugs and styling out a disaster with panache, rather than letting disaster befall me.

For weeks I'd driven my Dad demented by reciting it down the phone. Mistakenly, he kept calling it my FedEx talk and I wished I *had* been delivering a parcel rather than a talk.

It wasn't long before one of the TEDx assistants arrived to fetch me. She miked me up and advised me to stay stageside until it was my turn. From the wings, I watched one of the speakers, a poised, elegant Greek goddess, talk to a rapt audience about seizing the day. At that point, I realised I'd forgotten my water. I asked the assistant to help and she went scuttling off, but already the Greek glamazon was walking off the stage to great applause.

The compere was introducing me. I couldn't help noticing she had ditched the controversial intro I had suggested about Michael Stone (the Stormont terrorist) being one of my favourite performance artists in favour of something a bit more watery.

I stepped on to applause, the odd encouraging whoop, and took my place on the 'red dot'. I started reciting my lines – a few laughs came and I began to grow in confidence. I kept looking for faces I knew, faces that smiled at me. Gratifyingly, Ana Matronic kept snorting with laughter. I felt in control of the audience and at that exact moment of course I forgot my words, and had to frantically scramble through my cue cards. Once more, I resumed.

When I saw my arms moving, they seemed out of sync with the motionless audience. It was all very surreal. I couldn't feel my own body. I forgot the next sentence, but once more I rallied and delivered a line that earnt a resounding cheer. As my voice rose up through the marble columns I felt in total command. But, knowing I had a very wordy section ahead, a terrible thirst came on me. My words felt clamped to the roof of my mouth like I'd just smoked twenty joints. I was literally ready to lurch off the stage in pursuit of water. Everything went into slow motion; my tongue went as large and floppy as a camel's. A girl in the third row seemed to lick her lips in sympathy with me. I suddenly remembered how an actress friend of mine had once lost it on stage when she'd spotted a nurse who'd recently given her a smear test sitting in the front row, so I told myself not to look at anyone, to look up towards the lights. Just then, I forgot my lines again.

I could hear a slow ironic handclap from the back of the audience. I looked for encouragement in the front rows, but even Ana Matronic was looking at the floor, the way you do when something is too much of a car crash to confront. I set off again and managed to work up a bit of passion and pull a couple of final titters out of the audience, but when I stumbled off the stage the reception was a lot more muted than the one that had greeted me.

The stage manager, who'd engulfed the Greek goddess in rapturous, camp kisses, didn't meet my eye, pretending to be busy with some sort of mike malfunction on the next speaker.

I headed back to the green room. Oh, god, the hideosity of it all!

The previous speakers were buzzing, all of them apparently trending on Twitter.

I was downing a bottle of water as the American guy Dan arrived with fresh platters.

'I thought your talk was great,' he enthused. 'Except for the bit about California. We're not all like that, you know!'

I laughed because my talk had just dissed Dan's home state for being the hub of faux life-transforming self-helpery. He had a terrific smile. I guessed he was fit under his shirt. Of course, you never could tell. I once met a man on a train who was wearing a hat. I'd really liked him and had agreed to go on a date with him. During our date, he finally took off his hat to reveal a bald cranium as big as a giant lightbulb.

At the break, the organiser, Camilla, reassured me that my pauses would later be edited out on YouTube, so I began to feel a bit happier. To be honest, I was just relieved I could toss my cue cards in the bin.

I was soon sitting in the front row, enjoying the rest of the talks. A 'digital leader' was advocating a switch-off of all social media outside work hours which seemed a bit of a mixed message, especially as I'd just watched her ferociously tweeting in the green room. She was full of excruciatingly peppy soundbites like 'you're the captain of make it happen'. Then came an ex-newscaster who talked of upholding the sisterhood. I found myself nodding and clapping, really into her views. It occurred to me I should be more generous to the other TEDx women and much less jealous.

The final speaker was Ana Matronic. She entranced to tumultuous applause and took to the dot, unwavering as she tilted her chin skyward like an Olympic athlete on a podium. She talked about her obsession with robots. At one point there was an ever-so-slight glitch in the flow, but the ghost in the machine wheeled back into action and she exited to the same fervent devotion. Young women buzzed around her, getting her to sign their programmes. I wished my own talk had been as professional, but I consoled myself with the fact that genius always has its sloppy moments. I was sure some genius had invented a pithy quote to match that thought, but of course I couldn't think of one.

I managed to get a lift with the lesbian speaker to the after-show party in Bullitt. Thinking of the sisterhood I told her she'd been great, and I wasn't lying either. She was on such a high she kept taking the wrong turn, so we were the last to arrive by miles.

Bullitt was one of those showy bars with a drinks menu thicker than a novel. I'd been there once before and had been handed a glass of gin and tonic that looked like rat droppings were floating in it. It turned out to be juniper berries. Tonight, however, there were a hundred free cocktails waiting for us. I was feeling brand new, having just shed a kilo of words from my brain. I joined Ana Matronic for a while. A tattoo peeked out from under the sleeve of her dress like some sort of cyber company brand name. I touched her white skin just to check that she was human and not some beautiful sexbot. She took it in her stride, but seemed surprised. I'd forgotten how touchy Americans are about being touched. I once was being ignored by an air hostess on United Airlines when I lightly tapped her on the arm. 'Excuse me, but you do not violate my personal space,' she had responded accusingly, and I'd cowered back in my seat, everyone looking at me like I was a mile-high rapist.

The digital leader was telling us how well she was doing since she went bankrupt. I guessed she was mentioning it because it made her rise seem all the more spectacular. Funnily enough, I'd googled Camilla a few weeks ago and she had been bankrupt too. If I could equal these high-flying women in any part of their CVs, I was pretty sure I could do the bankruptcy.

I went over to join Californian Dan at the bar. He was about six four, buff, blond and had a cute laugh that was a kind of a gruff giggle. His nose was too long to make him symmetrically good-looking but he had teasing eyes. He told me he was on a Mitchell scholarship and was studying world religions – this immediately made me view him in a much less sexual light – but he added he'd been in the US Marines, which made me review him in a highly-sexual light. I swear I could feel the heat of his body a foot away.

We kept knocking back our cocktails. At one point, we fished the slices of freeze-dried pear out of our glasses and tried to eat them, but they were rock-hard, so we spat them out.

'Call yourself a tough US marine,' I teased.

'Call yourself a public speaker.'

'I don't actually. Anyway, what's the point of having perfect Californian teeth if you can't crunch a pear?'

We were enjoying our love song banter, drinking more and more. A couple of girls saw us laughing and came over.

'Look at the state of that,' one girl said to me, mopping up the mangled pear from the counter into a napkin. 'Imagine you slinging it there with all your germs.'

It was a crude attempt to impress Dan with her housekeeping skills while dissing me for my slovenliness, but I just ignored it. Instead I told them how I'd prepared for my TEDx talk. I'd got my friend to shine her kitchen lights into my eyes to replicate the glare of the lights in Stormont's Great Hall. I'd also got her to laugh and gasp at extremely inappropriate moments during my talk to make sure the audience wouldn't faze me. The girls guffawed, and Dan was so charmed by my ludicrous account he turned his body from the girls back towards me. The girls drifted away.

He was telling me about a woman he'd stopped seeing recently because she was too keen.

'She was a redhead like you,' he said.

'Well, you know us redheads,' I replied, telling him all about how we feel more pain, more heat, more cold than normal people, how we're so much more tuned in to every physical sensation. 'And it's not only pain we're alive to, but the intensity of every pleasure,' I rhapsodised and I could feel the slow burn of my words drawing him in. I could almost smell him, and it had been so long since I'd been with a man with that scent of earthy truffles and sweet apple vinegar sweat.

Ana Matronic was leaving and I joined the rush to say goodbye. She squeezed my hand and promised to look up my articles and read them. Of course, she wasn't going to, she was just being her ever consummate professional self, but I appreciated the thought.

Dan brought me over another cocktail. I usually prefer beers to spirits and they were hitting me hard.

'What? I'm hardly getting a buzz off these,' said Dan.

I didn't know what it was – the cocktails or the adrenaline high wearing off. But I wanted to take Dan back to mine, so I kept on chatting brightly. I noticed his body tilting away from mine – it was only a fraction but it felt like a door had been reopened and the deal was not quite sealed.

'Sorry, I'm just noticing that girl at the bar,' he said, distracted. 'She reminds me of my sister.'

I glanced across. The girl looked about twenty two. She was stunning, with long, dark curly hair, a hint of Arabic in her. I wondered how she could possibly resemble a relative of Dan's when he was so blond, tall and pale.

'She keeps looking over,' he said.

I quickly started jabbering about how I was heading to a conference the next day and would have to leave soon. I was trying to get him to come home with me, but he was a kid in a sweet shop – I was pear drops or plain liquorice, and the new girl was the sherbert fizz.

Her friend was walking towards us, locking her sights on me. She was pretty, black-skinned and in her early twenties.

'Hey. Let me introduce myself. I'm Jasmin,' she said. 'My friend and I were just wondering if we could join you?'

'Yeah. Why not?' said Dan before I could say a word.

'Cool. I'll go and get her then,' Jasmin beamed as she left.

'They planned it,' explained Dan, the US Marine in him detecting their strategic manoeuvres. 'She was sent over to split us up. She's talking to you, so I'll be free for her friend.'

I didn't know what to say. Before I knew it, we were all sitting down at a table together. Jasmin was telling me she was originally from Mogadishu and had come over to Belfast as a child. She was interesting but I was acutely aware of Dan and his girl chatting away next to me. I kept glancing across at him, his knees as square as boulders, the way his jacket cut into his neck muscle, the balls of his thumbs as big as grenades. I felt like I was on some bizarre double date. It wasn't fair. I'd entertained him with my wit for two hours, only to have him brutally snaffled in a pincer movement by a much younger and, importantly, more sober woman. I was Gen X, Gen Sex, outmanoeuvred by a couple of post-millennials! So much for the sisterhood!

But then it was his fault, not theirs. He could easily have chosen to stay with me. And even then I couldn't blame him, because although tonight I may have had the words, looks always trump words.

'Excuse me,' I said to Jasmin, getting to my feet and heading to the bar.

It was closing and the last of the speakers were leaving.

'I really liked your talk,' I told the ex-newscaster who'd spoken of the sisterhood.

Standing there, saying goodbye to the others, I suddenly remembered my graduation day when I had been on the stage shaking hands with Dame Margot Fonteyn, and I'd looked down into the audience, expecting to see my mother gazing proudly at me, only to find her looking at someone else. My mum was always dazzled by other people. Even now, whenever I pointed out what great jobs my friends had, my mother would always say 'yes, but they're personality-plus,' in a tone of such finality I was left in no doubt that I was personality-deficient. No wonder I kept trying to promote myself with the vigour of a Linenhall Street sex worker.

I said goodbye to the lesbian speaker. She was still thrilling about how TEDxBoston had retweeted her. I imagined TEDx ringing me up from Silicon Valley and asking me to deliver a brand new talk in LA. 'Sure thing,' I'd say nonchalantly, 'send the deets to my peops.'

As I put on my coat, one of the evening's soundbites about 'future-proofing your life' filtered back to me. I didn't see how it was possible, but everyone around me seemed to be planning their lives down to the last detail.

Dan bounded up.

'Hey, are you leaving?'

'Yes. Are you going to go home with that girl tonight?'

'Yeah, I might as well.'

'Go for it,' I said, kissing him goodbye.

Then I went out into the night. It was raining, but the beauty was I no longer cared about my hair.

PINE NEEDLES

I

A stick of light moved across the floor through a chink in the curtains that quivered from time to time by the open window. A pigeon was cooing from somewhere above, an amplified eerie sound like the hoot of a monkey in the jungle, and a coughing fit could be heard from within the neighbouring apartment. Erin sat down on the bed and fell back, arms outstretched, submitting to the heat of the Prague summer. She turned her head to the side and watched Koji sitting at the desk. He was leafing through a box of photos.

'Are you bored again?'

She heard the accusation in his voice and sat up.

'No, just hot. What are you looking at?'

'My evidence.'

She was relieved to see a small smile, and smiled too as she often did at his formal turn of speech.

Koji was as tall as her, not as slender, but finely built all the same, almost gamine, those black petal-shaped eyes slanting above the wide cheekbones, a swarthy skin tone turned pale from lack of sunlight, delicate lips pressed tight in concentration like a child. He was wearing her trainers, the ones that had become so worn inside they hurt her feet. They were navy with white rubber soles and he wore them as slippers as he didn't like the rubber to be dirtied in the dust of the street.

He came to sit down beside her and she made room for him, taking care not to sit on the pillow. He had told her in his country, Japan, it was the seat of the gods. She took care so often now; such matters had become habitual.

'It's Cambodia,' he said softly, and she looked at a black and white photo of people laughing in a temple next to a headless statue of Buddha.

'It's beautiful.'

'Refugees. A long time ago. It may be beautiful but never forget that these things belong to tragedy.'

'I've never seen any of your photos of Bosnia.'

'I threw them all in the fire. I don't want to remember.'

He cleared his throat, touched it lightly with his fingertips which then fluttered up to his face. 'No, all my friends in Asia say to me I have not changed since this time. They have an expression of extreme disbelief when they look at me. Everyone says I haven't aged.'

An odd sensation of unreality came over her. From her seat at the edge of the bed, she could see into the shadowy hall. Behind the Buddha cup was a mirror he'd covered entirely with a scarf, the reason being that he was afraid of seeing ghosts. While she easily dismissed this as superstitious nonsense, there were moments when she sensed immortality and the supernatural living in his beliefs.

'So,' he went on, looking back at the photo. 'We will go to Cambodia when we go to Asia and we can live in Japan for longer. I want to show you a new world. You know, I can't feel real lives here in Europe, everyone is living on a ruin. Prague is a trifling place. There's no god here, only the dollar. The west is finished. I think you know well now.'

He reached across her, and slammed the door of the cupboard. She knew she annoyed him by not closing everything tightly. She left doors and drawers open, almost as a statement that the flat was ridiculously tiny; openings provided extra pockets of breath, a kind of freedom in the tight order preferred by Koji. Was it any wonder they got on each other's nerves? A small kitchen, a miniature hall, one cramped living room with the less than roomy bed shoved against the wall (thank god they were both slim), the desk and chair only a short bound away. The toilet and shower were off the living room and the water was heated by a gas boiler that kept going out. She called it the death trap and wouldn't go near it with a match, which didn't impress him as she was perfectly willing for him to take the risk. She lay back again, listening to the crisp sound of Koji leafing through the photos, crooking her arm to prop up the back of her head, feeling the blood pump across her skull against her forearm.

In the beginning she had loved that he'd said the word busy meant nothing to him. Of course she admired him for writing novels which had already been commissioned, and for taking photographs of the passages (he pronounced it the French way, pass*ages*) in Prague for his dealer, but he always had time for her and she appreciated that. It was now, however, her third month after moving in with him, and his artistic activity had reached a period of stagnancy. It bothered her that he wasn't getting on with his life, as if he was using her as an experience, already doubting she would stay with him. Of course, there had been the afternoon she'd gone out for a walk only to be driven back early by the heat to find him sitting writing, drinking wine, and he had been angry at the interruption, but when she'd offered to go out again for another walk he wouldn't hear of it. She was beginning to understand that Buddhism meant a life of inaction, far removed from the Protestant work ethic with which she had grown up. She shifted, thinking she might burst if she didn't say what was on her mind.

'So, when do you think we can go to Asia?'

He looked at her with irritation. 'You must not want always to hurry up. I said in maybe three months. I am waiting big money from the gallery owner.'

She took a deep breath. For days now she'd been wanting to pin him down. She didn't want to stay in limbo like this. 'It's just I'm not working now and I haven't much money left.'

He clutched his head. 'I said I'd take care of it. You, you fear too much. You are too careful of the future by which you destroy the present. Sometimes you fire bullets into my head.'

She cursed under her breath. 'Bullets! It was only a simple question.' She could hear her own annoyance under the attempted reason. 'Why can't I have some share of the decision?'

'It's your character. You are nervous. I told you, if you cannot wait, then go home. You can't feel free. You think too much with your brains and not with your feelings.' He stood up, angrily. 'So, go back to your parents' house. Go on. You will flap back like a big bird. Your evacuation place. Always it's easy for you because you can go back to your parents, then you go to another country to teach, find another man, then you get bored and go home again. A merry-go-round but as you get older you'll find that no one will love you. You will be forty and you will wake up alone still in these foreign countries, some sad, old teacher. You don't want that, do you?'

'No, I don't.'

'You are like a child who eats a little of everything.' He put his hands at either side of his head to block off the side view. 'In fact you're like a horse, you can't see anything around you.'

'Well, at least a horse can go forward.'

His face was a fury. 'You are very impolite. You are stupid. It's art. Do you think it is like university with schedules? My articles, my photographs. You think I must hurry up? Is life an exam? You are just a student. You should go to the front line and see what life is.'

'Look, I'm sorry,' she said, defensively, wanting him to halt.

'I don't want to hear any English from now on. I'm tired of caring for you. You can speak to me in French. Everyone in the world thinks the English are egotists. That's why nobody likes them. I don't want to speak English.'

'I'm not English.'

He didn't respond. His eyes were cold and she was afraid. He muttered in his own language and went into the bathroom. She could hear him splashing water over his face.

When he came out, she said to him calmly, 'I was angry there. I didn't mean to insult you.'

She expected a further onslaught of words and was relieved to hear softness. 'No, I like your way. Sometimes I think my way is no good either.' He shook his head to one side as if to remove water from one ear. 'I went to see the art dealer yesterday, he gave me a headache. I know the truth. They're waiting for me to die, then they can sell my photos for great money.'

'You didn't tell me you went.'

'I didn't want to make you nervous.'

'But you can tell me anything.'

'I don't want to fight you. That was how it was with my

151

wife. We were always hard fighting.' He sat, legs crossed, his hands folded tightly into his lap in an expression of suffering, and she put her hand gently onto the back of his.

'I hate to fight.'

'I want you now to go slow, have no plans, be flexible. Now is not a time for "must".'

'I know, I'm impatient.'

'Sometimes I think you should go home. I'm not a good or kind man. Sometimes I am frightened by myself.'

'I don't want to go home.'

'That makes me happy.' He smiled. 'I need you,' he said, abruptly pulling himself up, remembering that this word had sparked a previous argument. 'No, I mean I want you to stay with me for longer.'

'I will.' She checked her watch. 'Isn't it time for your student?'

His private lesson was due at four and he got up. 'No, I'll cancel it. Let's drink some beer, relax.'

She said nothing, but found it typical of him. She would have found it good to have a breathing space but each occasion after they argued, he cancelled his arrangements almost to prove how much he loved her and to profit by the renewed softness of the atmosphere.

II

A frenetic hammering came from neighbouring apartments, as it often did in the late afternoon when Czech mothers were in the kitchen flattening pork into escalopes.

Koji stood at the peeling window, staring at the apartment block opposite.

'I would like to hit the Czech moles as they pop out their heads.' He imitated the game, moving his arm energetically and striking with an imaginary hammer.

'Bam. Bam. You know that game?'

Erin laughed with him and he shook his head as if bemused by the Czechs. '*Baka*,' he said. 'Stupid. Maybe I'll go out later and take photos,' he said, turning to her. 'The light will be good. I want to capture the beautiful evening light, the yellow like Rembrandt's paintings.'

He stared over her head into the middle distance of the off-white wall, and suddenly she could see the yellow ochre of his vision.

'You want to go out alone?'

'No. I want to show you that there is luck lying in the dungpool.'

'Maybe we could have dinner somewhere in town?' she asked hopefully, and a vision of Prague sprang into her mind with its well-hidden bars hosting poetry readings and jam sessions, while the Americans downed absinthe in the background. Oh sure, at the time of meeting Koji she'd already become tired of all that. Six months of teaching in a city awash with the most pretentious of expats had left her jaded with the whole scene, but it now seemed she had moved to an entirely different country.

'But I'm cooking the noodles and pork tonight,' he said with an expression of hurt.

A strange feeling came over her, breathing life into an old memory of standing outside a pub in Galway. On that occasion she'd found the door locked, though she could see from the window the froth-pale faces of the people inside. She knocked hard but no one came to the door and after a minute she left, feeling as though she was in an unreal world where nobody was aware of her existence.

In the beginning she had found him so kind and thoughtful. In many ways he still was. Had she been in love back then? Yes, but more and more she was confused as to what love was. He had been very quick to extract a declaration of love from her. Yes, *extracted* was the word. It had almost been a case of 'if you don't say you love me now, you will never see me again.' For someone who didn't hurry, he had been very fast.

She hadn't planned to move in with him. She was informed on the Sunday night that the next morning she'd have to vacate her apartment for ten days while new plumbing was installed. His first reaction when she arrived at his door was displeasure. The desk was spread with his notebooks, a tumbler of red wine sitting on some pages like a paperweight. After he'd put these things away, he'd been happy.

'Perhaps we should go and see Otto soon,' Koji mused. 'I told him we would go in July.'

An opportunity for her own space sprang to mind. 'You could go alone any time if you like.'

'But I want us to go together.'

'Ok,' she agreed quickly. 'I don't mind going.'

It was a lie. In the early days they'd gone together to Otto and Lenka's. Otto was a thin, besuited businessman with a hectoring manner in contrast with his soft-spoken, nurturing wife. Erin remembered bitterly how, catching her alone for a minute, Otto had asked her about her future plans and she'd replied that she might teach elsewhere or go back to her native country. Days later this conversation resurfaced in an argument.

'Even Otto says you don't love me,' stated Koji. 'You didn't mention me in your plans. "Why are you with such a cold woman?" he asked me.'

'Well, you and I have never discussed plans,' Erin reasoned. 'Besides, did you never think Otto's out to make trouble for us?'

'He's a friend. He speaks the truth, as he sees it at least.'

'No, he's jealous because you do art while he must do business. Plus, he prefers you single because it is clear, honey, you're still a little bit in love with his wife and that would make a man like Otto feel good about himself.'

Yes, it was better they saw no one. Another time she'd told an English couple who worked in her school about Koji and his experiences as a war photographer, and they'd expressed such eagerness to meet him she'd arranged a night out in the pub. The couple for all their prior enthusiasm had been very silent while he graphically recounted a story about an ex-IRA man killing himself in Bosnia by Russian roulette and the evening descended into awkwardness. Back at the apartment Koji had plunged into self-castigation.

'I wasted my life,' he bemoaned. 'You were right when you said a war photographer sucks experiences, changes nothing, profits from misfortune. Maybe it was better after all to be like those English people.'

But Erin also suspected it was payback for her dislike of Otto.

Bosnia, she knew in particular, had been a traumatic experience for Koji. He'd photographed an impromptu execution of a Serb by Croatian soldiers and had managed to pass the film to a group of villagers. The Croatian soldiers, drunk on plum brandy, had then beaten him severely, almost blinding him in one eye and damaging his throat. But for the intervention of their captain, he would have been killed. He'd received counselling but the nightmares wouldn't go away, and writing about his experiences perpetuated the problem. He once had asked incredulously 'how does a writer like Frederick Forsyth write nothing about the trauma? He must surely have nightmares.' She had explained to him about British sangfroid and he had sat in bemusement, shaking his head.

Erin twisted the cap off the bottle of sparkling water and Koji smiled.

'I want to swim in that crispy water.' He raised his chin, closed his eyes and put his arms up in the air, waving them gently as though floating, and she laughed. The heat was stifling, pinking the bodies of the people walking by down at street level. In Czech the word for July was Červenec meaning redder, following on from June which was Červen, meaning red.

'I have an idea,' said Koji impulsively. 'Remember I said I wanted to go to Český Těšín to take photos of the black market?' He paused while Erin nodded. 'Well, I think we should go. A trip would be good for us.'

She lit with pleasure. 'I'd love to go. When?'

'Well, not tomorrow. The next day. Time we moved a little.' He squeezed the non-existent fat on his stomach. 'There is nothing I despise more than writers with fat bodies.'

'It will be so good to see something different.'

'We can both take pictures. You can take the Konica. It's a very good camera to begin with,' he explained, warming to the idea. He walked to the cupboard, taking out the Konica and sat down next to her, pressing it into her hand. 'Here, it's a present for you. I want to help you find your expression. Then you won't be bored. I can teach you everything. The best art comes from pure motives. Beauty is everything. Too many so-called artists try to shock and I call it filth. They are jealous. Some photographers say of me, "Look at him. Why does he make beauty out of war?" But me, I say why do they make ugliness out of peace?' He looked at her intently. 'I am sure you'll have a very good artistic sense.'

'Well.' She felt his hand move up her forearm.

'Do you want to take a shower?'

'Why not?' she said and they both smiled. She went into the bathroom and it was on her mind to remind him he'd probably now miss the yellow evening light, but, after all, that was his business and it didn't matter.

She peeled off her clothes. The tightness of her jeans had

left heated red marks around her stomach. She took off her ring and it had left a reddish band around her finger. She stepped into the shower. Before sex they both took showers. He always wanted her fresh smelling, and it had embarrassed her the one time he had complained. The boiler flame roared into action this time, but the black heads of matches still lay beside the tap from that morning, the charcoaled fragments reminding her of dead ants.

The water from the shower seemed almost to be singing in her ears, blocking out any other sound, and she took advantage of it to whisper, low in case Koji might hear 'I want to go home, I want to go home.' It meant nothing really – it had often been a habit of hers, and when she got back to her home city she would say the same. She didn't know what home meant, whether it was peace of mind or comfort or a room alone or a state of unconsciousness.

She stopped the whispering, took up the soap and began to scrub hard.

III

The words of *The Tibetan Book of the Dead* entered her soul like a programme of brightly coloured symbols downloading effortlessly within her mind. It was a world of compassion, light and air.

'Nirvana is the state of a flame being blown out,' she read. 'Do not delight in the dim blue light of the human realm. Delight in the yellow.'

And she remembered Koji telling her his brown eyes were better than blue at seeing in the dark. Neither did his eyes water like hers in the strong sunlight.

She found herself seduced by words such as bliss, realms, enlightenment and impermanence, but most importantly she'd discovered that the meaning of life was to attain perfection. The meaning of life was to break with habit and become a god. The book spoke to her. It reassured her that her life of travel was part of the scheme of things, as the soul was rootless and without end. Sometimes while she walked around Prague it saddened her as she knew the city was destined to shrink and blur in her memory, but now she knew to embrace transience.

She read aloud, her accent conforming strangely to the beauty as it would to a different language. 'We are like rocks weathered into beautiful forms.'

She suddenly glanced at the clock. It was a rare occasion when Koji was absent from the apartment, and she wanted to make the most of it. She had thought of taking a walk but it was early afternoon and the window revealed a sapping sky of mountainous hazes. Before meeting Koji, she remembered, she'd packed so much into her months in Prague. There had been the Czech man, the Russian, the American who'd invited her to go travelling with him ... her life had been a blur of flicking pages. The day came back to her when, as a fresh-faced graduate, she was sacked from her job sub-editing a magazine and, breathing the air deep outside the office, she'd decided never to trap herself in a conventional career again.

She closed the fiery orange cover of the book and set it down carefully like a worker laying the first tile. Since being with him she had learnt a great deal. He'd brought to her a new world of the saffron-robed monks who travelled continents in their minds, who could catch flies with their chopsticks; he'd shown her the paintings of Modigliani, the prints of Izis and was beginning to teach her his language and photography. She felt guilty she was giving little in return.

She stood up and stretched. A sound soon came of a key in the door, a tiny clockwise click giving notice that he was back.

IV

After dinner Koji moved the plates away and shook the crumbs from the tablecloth. He took out his first cigarette of the day and lit it, sniffing the smoke like a sensualist. He passed the packet to Erin.

'Go on. I know you can't smoke at home with your family, but take one. You are free here.'

She accepted one, letting him light it for her.

'Good meal?' he beamed. He raised to his lips one of the litre bottles of Budvar sitting on the table.

'Very good.'

'Hot meals, hot body.'

'Tomorrow in Český Těšín let's eat trout in a restaurant. Well, it's not sushi but it's the next best thing.'

'Yes, trout is good.' He rocked back on his chair and opened the fridge door, setting in the plate with the remaining tomatoes and gherkins. 'Ah,' he said, luxuriating in the coldness of the open fridge at his back.

'Maybe we should hibernate in there over the summer,' Erin joked.

'Yes, but we'll have to buy in more beer first. I love beer.'

'I know. Why don't you pour some beer into Buddha's cup instead of water?'

He laughed happily. 'He might like it.'

'Well, why not? Wine represents Christ's body.'

'Yes, but I don't like the Christian god. I already told you I think he is jealous. He wants to stop people having fun. It's always don't do this, don't do that.'

She smiled weakly, not wanting to add fuel to one of his common themes.

'I forgot to tell you,' he exclaimed, tapping his thigh. 'I dreamed about you last night. There was a boy at the bus stop standing beside you. The boy was about four years old and had black hair. You didn't recognise him and he didn't recognise you, but he was just looking at you.'

'Strange dream.'

'Then I realised that boy was me reincarnated.' His eyes had suddenly filled with tears.

'Oh.' She was shocked, and her own eyes filled. Before living with Koji she had never really known that about herself, that she was able so fast to mirror other people's emotions.

He pulled his sleeves up his arms, his lips pursed. 'It's ok. I know well my condition. Dying to me is like changing clothes.'

She picked at the label on her bottle without looking at him.

'You were moving around a lot in your sleep last night.' His voice was sharper, almost accusing.

'Yes, I like to be well done on both sides,' she answered lightly. She took another gulp of beer, holding it in her mouth, letting it go flat, trying to savour it. It was unpleasantly strong to the taste, so she swallowed quickly. She thought of the effect of each further gulp of beer on her body. It was no wonder that after two litre bottles every night, she felt lethargic, muzzy-headed.

'Shall we go next door?'

'Yes.'

'You haven't finished your beer.'

There was less than a third in the bottle. 'All beer does in this heat is make me tired.'

Koji was angry. 'We must never leave what nature gives to us.'

'Nature doesn't give it to us. We ferment it and put it into bottles too big to finish. Why do you think there are so many fat Americans waddling around Prague?'

'You are saying wrong about nature. In Asia we say

every grain of rice is the blood of a farmer. That's why in our country we don't waste.'

'I don't like waste either.'

'You don't understand well. The stomach to the Samurai is the holy place. We say if you are hungry, you can't fight. I hope that one day you will starve and then you will appreciate.'

Having delivered the killer blow he stared at her face, then put up a hand in apology. 'Sorry, sorry.' His own face had transformed to smiles. 'Sometimes I am too hard with you. I forget your ways are different. I must have patience.'

'It's ok.'

'No, it isn't. I remember I was a child and I told my brother he was *baka*. He was slow, he had to go to a special school. I can't remember what he did to me but then I went to my mother and complained to her, "My brother is stupid." She said to me, "Stupid is lovely." I never forgot that. Stupid is lovely.'

She nodded but the conversation was boring her. She had heard the story before as she had done with most of his stories. She picked up her beer bottle and emptied it down the sink.

'I'll wash up now. You go next door and relax.'

V

Koji was sitting cross-legged on the bed, vigorously wiping his Leica with a cloth. 'This Leica is my weapon of expression,' he told Erin. 'But I know my final purpose will be to make films. I want them blue, very beautiful. Light blue. I want it to be ... entrancing.'

Erin didn't look up from selecting underwear from the set of drawers.

'I don't have another clean t-shirt.'

'You can borrow mine.'

'Thanks. We're always cross dressing, aren't we?'

He shook his head to one side. 'Maybe I'm thinking tomorrow isn't good for going. We could wait another day.'

She'd been expecting this, but she wasn't going to let him wriggle off the hook this time. Always this policy of wretched containment, a constant pandering to his whims. Flies were buzzing round the electric light that glowed like a bright stamen surrounded by the flowering of the lampshade.

'Come on. What's the point of waiting? Tomorrow will be an adventure.'

'Ah, yes. One more in a long line of adventures before you go back to mother.'

She turned away. It seemed he was always jealous of her family. When he'd told her the story of how his mother had committed suicide without leaving a note, without leaving a reason, she had begun to understand why he railed so much against her relationship with her parents.

'You are a migratory bird,' he said teasingly. 'You can't stay still anywhere. I keep telling you, you must be free.'

'Be free of attachment and aversion,' she quoted back at him from *The Tibetan Book of the Dead*. 'You want me to be free, yet keep saying you want me to stay with you. Your desire and these words are a contradiction.'

'I'm not that person!' He looked shocked. 'I said to you many times to go if you want. I only want you to feel natural, but you can't help it. Fear and struggle are illusions in your mind. One day I want you to go to the front line too. You will see. You are like Susan Sontag. She came to Bosnia to smell the atmosphere like it was the Spanish Civil War. We were all staying at the Holiday Inn in Sarajevo and every day I went to the front line while she stayed behind and wrote. One day I said to her, "If you have so much sympathy for the Bosnians, take a rifle and go to the front line." "It's not my work," she told me. "It's not my work." She made a fortune from selling her books. And I made money too.'

He tailed off into a bitter silence and she was relieved he'd spiralled once more into the past. She didn't want to further jeopardise the trip the following day. But why couldn't he see the ridiculousness of a life spent in inaction discussing a former life of action? She understood his need for a stable home life, but such a life was too dull for her. It struck her suddenly that they had only drunk beer together, and it was as if he compartmentalised wine as a creative tool for his writing, shutting her out even from that pleasure.

He recommenced cleaning the Leica in his lap and let out a sigh. His eyelashes were downturned like pine needles.

She bent over her bag, putting in the carefully folded t-shirts. Her hair hung down over her cheeks, and she could see it was red, almost as red as ever but with faint peppery strands.

'Trifling,' she heard him mutter to himself as the cloth flicked over the camera. 'Trifling.'

After a while, she felt a pat on her shoulder.

'I'm sorry,' he said. 'Let's not argue again. I don't want to argue.'

'Neither do I,' and she was glad of his smile.

VI

The train for Český Těšín left at six. Koji rose an hour before her at four, as he wanted to cook himself breakfast and didn't like to hurry. She sometimes wondered how he'd managed to get to the front line in time. As they left the apartment block, she put a bag of rubbish in the bin and held open the lid for him, not realising the bag in his hand contained freshly-made sandwiches. She laughed at herself but he was peeved at the misunderstanding.

It was only five thirty, yet there was a great burst of morning light from behind the buildings, and the sun alchemised the dirt on the tram windows into a golden-particled haze. The tram was already busy with commuters, and began to hurtle down the hill from Žižkov towards the Old Town, revealing the snake of the Prague roofs, the red-scaled and spiny writhing backs, windows wide open like gills gasping for air, the round gable windows eyeing the shadowy light. Erin could remember exploring Prague the previous year. How wonderful it had felt back then! The breeze from the windows of the tram refreshed her face like freedom. She caught sight of a girl observing them from under long, mascaraed eyelashes. It flattered her that this girl found them worthy of being watched. She was often alert to people's gazes and it made her proud to be with such a beautiful man.

They were running late, and had to sprint through the station. The wheels of suitcases screeched all around them, like birds scattering from the pound of their feet. They made their train with moments to spare.

Koji sat down opposite her. He mentioned coldly that they should have left themselves more time. She said something cheery and pulled out a book, dividing her time between contemplation of its pages and the dry fields of pale powder rimmed with the red smile of poppies. Shuttling further and further from Prague, they began to pass small villages wedged between hills of wild-headed pines. The ground by the rail tracks was a fiery Persian carpet, thick with red and orange needles. From time to time she glanced obliquely at Koji, not wanting to catch his eye. He was sitting with his hand draped protectively over the front of his haversack. The hand was delicate, curved at the wrist like a swan's neck, downturned and sad, but she was determined not to let his mood spoil her day.

VII

A long queue was waiting at the border between the Czech Republic and Poland. The passport control unexpectedly traversed a shopping street crowded with black market stalls of food, goods and alcohol. Only a small section of the border crossing bore the cover of a white tarpaulin, and most shoppers stood in the full glare of the sun, arms wilting under great gourds of shopping bags.

'You stupid woman!' Koji was shouting. 'You want that we are robbed?'

Erin had gone to take the passports out of her money belt, inadvertently revealing a wad of folded money.

'We won't get robbed. We'll be careful.'

'They watch us here. Maybe you don't look foreign but I do.'

There was a fifteen minute wait to get across the border. The guards in particular tarried over Koji's passport and, anticipating problems, he explained he didn't need a visa. After another inspection, they passed it back to him disinterestedly as though their thought processes were as faded by the sun as their uniforms.

Koji wore his camera round his neck but hadn't taken any photos. Pulling into Český Těšín, they had seen the blisteringly ugly white panelaks in the suburbs give way to a fairly picturesque town centre but neither of them were impressed. He wanted to see an old graveyard he'd read about in the guidebook, so Erin stopped a passerby and asked him the way in English but he seemed unsure and spoke Polish to her with glittering, lustful eyes.

'Leave him,' snapped Koji hysterically. 'Ask a woman. Can't you ask?'

'If you don't like it, you ask then,' she retorted.

She walked away from him, thinking of returning to Prague alone, yet she knew that would cause even more trouble.

'You don't know well,' he said fiercely.

As they continued up the street, the words 'stupid is lovely' would not leave her head.

VIII

They'd plumped in the absence of choice to have lunch in some tacky touristy place with red Vladivar umbrellas in a courtyard that was a suntrap. The prices were high, but Koji insisted she should have a steak, although she compromised by choosing the cheapest one on the menu. Seeing this, he accused her of not having changed enough money.

She stared at the yellow-washed wall behind his head. Scaling its height were spindly creepers that looked like cracks in the plaster.

When the dishes arrived, she was dismayed.

'My god, I forgot what steak tartare was,' she exclaimed, looking at the mound of raw meat topped by egg.

'You are so impolite!' exploded Koji, throwing his cutlery onto his own dish. 'You point out my mistake, make me feel shame.'

'But it was my mistake to order it, not yours. You don't have to feel bad. I'm beginning to think you like feeling bad.'

His face twisted, a cluster of small, cruciform wrinkles bursting out around his eyes which appeared almost black in the bleached light of the courtyard.

'If you did this in Samurai times a man would run you through with a sword, then turn it on himself.'

'It's not Samurai times,' she remonstrated.

She stared at her plate in silence while he continued 'is it too much to ask you to do anything right? Can't you be an expert on anything?'

Tears sprang to her eyes. Something cracked inside her like the beginning of an earthquake, of something apocalyptic, the snap of a breaking relationship. 'You're so hard. It's unbearable. I can't take this anymore.'

His face changed, as though he had witnessed something shocking.

'I just want you to think before you act.'

'I can't go on with you. I'm sorry.'

He gulped, reaching across and transposing his dish with hers.

'I will eat yours. It's no problem.'

'No, it's ok.'

He dug into her dish with his fork and swallowed some. 'I like it. Tastes good and it is good for you.'

She chewed some of his omelette but it was bland. Suddenly she desired some of the steak tartare. She shouldn't have made a fuss. She needed food right now; it would make her stronger, and she reached across to his side of the table and took a forkful. It was surprisingly good.

'Do you want to go back to Prague?' His face was worried.

'No. We're here now. I want to enjoy here.' She spoke firmly, a decision already having been made.

'I went too far,' he said, a sob catching in his throat.

IX

The heavy windows of the pub swung inwards and the wind gusted the ash out of the ashtray, but Koji scarcely blinked.

'Last year when I was in Paris it all came back,' he was telling her. 'When I was in Bosnia I tried to die. I went to the front line, risked many things, but god wouldn't take me. And even now sometimes I feel like dying when I see the sun through the blinds in the morning. Sun coming up, mind going down. So, last year I was walking down the street in Paris when I heard a shout. I turn round, but no one's there. Then I look down and I see him! My old journalist friend from Bosnia. But he was a homeless man, eyes yellow with hepatitis, drinking from a bottle, big gulps like a baby in nursing and he cried when he saw me. We went to a park to talk, long talking, then some teenagers pass by and they call him dirty. "You don't know," I shout at them. "You haven't been to Bosnia."' He looked at her with anguish. 'Before meeting you I was like a doll without a soul. I went to see a Tibetan monk in February. He told me it was as if my soul was outside my soul. Like someone else was operating me, just like I was operating a camera. You see, I know well my condition.' He hit the side of his head with the hub of his hand. 'But it is no excuse. Sometimes I want to cry when I remember how I treated you.'

He stubbed out his cigarette, darting it into the ashtray, harpooning the fiery end that had broken off. The loss of deep contact with his eyes made her feel like she had just woken up from a hypnotic trance.

'The counsellor told me I have short-range vision, anger sometimes. It is worse since I am here. The Czechs remind me of Croatians.'

The barman picked up their empty glasses. He looked at them curiously out of grey eyes rimmed with pink. His hair was pulled back wetly into a ponytail. A rat's tail, thought Erin, stirring herself, awaking to the fact they weren't alone in the bar.

'Do you want another one?' Koji asked.

'No, thanks.'

'Yes, it's enough. You're tired now.'

'Tired of it all.'

'Me too. Very tired.' His eyes filled with tears. 'I know I

will never see my friend again. And all the time I think it could have been me like him committing slow suicide. Why not me?'

It struck her that the only times she'd seen him cry was because of someone he'd met on the front line, and never for a family member or loved one. He only cried thinking of himself in different earthly manifestations, and she was tired of his self pity and tired of his manipulation. It was as if he kept saying 'stay with me because it will only be a short time before I die.' Perhaps it was his only way of extracting tenderness from her.

'I think you must get more counselling.'

He nodded eagerly. 'Yes, I will go to Paris before we go to Japan.'

'I can't be with you when you're like that.'

'Already I am more stable than I was. I am taking the middle path. Now I'm looking straight ahead with my writing and photos.'

'I wish you would work instead of concentrating on me.'

'Please give me another chance. It's not too late, is it?'

She hesitated, scared by the pleading in his eyes, and looked away. Through the window she could see the gold of the sun clamber like a child into tight spaces between the lintels and alleyways of the street.

'No, it's not too late.'

They paid up and left the bar. In the street people were still walking along with heavy, clinking bags, the white gleam of tiredness under their eyes.

'You didn't get to take photos,' said Erin.

'No, but there is still tomorrow.' He seemed happy, comforted. To her mind, he had recovered his composure too soon.

In the hotel room, after their showers, he shuddered when he touched her. He whispered that love is heaven and kissed every part of her, every rib and every knot of muscle, relaxing her to her core, then putting his hands around her thighs and sinking deep. She stroked his hair, where it had been shaved at the back and sides of his head, loving the tingle on her fingers and he said nothing, although in his country it was the holy part of the body.

Afterwards, he quickly slid on his pyjama bottoms, shy again.

He fell asleep in renewed chastity, as if nothing had happened between them. She lay awake for a while, listening to his light breathing. He never snored. He had learnt to sleep silently from living with government forces in the jungle in Cambodia. His head tremored slightly, and she knew it was the nightmares. It brought back to her the memory of being woken up one night by a ferocious kick in the back, and he'd explained he'd been deep in a nightmare in which he was karate fighting an assailant. Sometimes it worried her that he would really hurt her one day.

She awoke to him pulling her hair in fun, and she pushed him away a little irritably. It was dusk.

'The innocent face of a sleeping you. There's nothing more appealing,' he whispered, and she patted his hand, feeling a surge of warmth towards him.

'It was a strong delight,' he told her tenderly. 'I had a thunderbolt down the back of my neck.'

They took another shower, hurrying a little because both were hungry for dinner. He was caring towards her, taking her clothes out of her bag and laying them neatly on the bed.

'You are beautiful,' he said, rubbing hand cream across the backs of his hands, while she dressed. 'You understand my mind. I trust you beyond anyone.'

She didn't reply. She felt smothered by the love he was distilling. All these emotions brewed out of idealisation and fear of loss. It was hard to breathe freely in the high-altitude air of the gods.

He knelt at her feet and wiped down her dusty white trainers with a hand towel.

'Try to be more beautiful,' he smiled and the white towel flicked back and forth.

X

On the train back to Prague the next afternoon, Erin was still tired. The weather had distinctly changed. It was hot, but the wind was strong and swirling and, up in the sky, the blue was chasing white clouds back down into the horizon as though herding them into an underground prison.

'You should sleep,' offered Koji, inviting her to lay her head on his lowered shoulder.

When she awoke it was to gales of laughter from the seats opposite. Three Czech girls were looking at her in fits of giggles.

'Was I snoring?' she asked Koji who was affecting innocence.

'No.' He decided to come clean. 'You had your mouth open so I stuck my finger in and took photos.' He smiled mischievously. 'The girls loved it.'

'I'm sure they did,' she laughed, liking him in this playful mood.

'You're not angry?'

'No.'

'That's why I love you. You are like a god,' he grinned but, seeing her face stiffen with tension, he immediately held up his hands in retraction. 'Sorry. Sorry. Bad joke.'

By the time they arrived in Prague he was subdued. Sitting on a bench outside the train station were a young couple, their legs intertwined, their backs leaning in towards one another, their heads like the two curves of a heart. Koji snapped them secretively without raising his camera to his eye.

'All the Czechs have love madness,' he commented darkly. 'They worship no god, so instead they look crazed into each other's eyes.'

They walked to the tram stop along a street of tall baroque buildings, the facades overlaid with ossiferous stone sculpted in the shape of fine garlands of leaves and flowers, tatty and tar-stained from the fumes of the city. Whole colonies of pigeons were roosting noisily up in the open attic windows. Erin shivered, as if privy to a glimpse of the oppressiveness that drove Hrabal, Palach, Masaryk, writers, heroes and politicians, to their suicidal end.

XI

Though the street was in shade now, the apartment was still hot, and Erin puffed her cheeks out, blowing her own breath over her face, flicking up her fringe. Air, warm and gritty, was entering in gusts from the window. She stood listening to Koji prepare tea in the kitchen and watching the flapping wings of paint on the window frame. She heard an exclamation from the hall, followed by Koji's steps, but she didn't rush to turn round.

'Strange,' he said, his eyes wide, setting down the tray. 'The water is gone from Buddha's cup.'

She gave a shrug. 'Oh, the heat must have evaporated it.'

'You think?' His voice was still tense.

'Well, I was thirsty when I came in,' she said lightly. 'Only joking!' she added when his brows lowered.

'It's very strange,' Koji pondered.

She watched as a loose sheet of paper blew from the desk onto the floor. The page was covered in the tiny indecipherable letters of his alphabet which he had transcribed for her. Her head was beginning to pound, so she took aspirin out of the drawer and washed two tablets down with tea.

'Let me see,' he said, moving beside her with concern. He rubbed his hands together and placed one across her forehead, concentrating, then asked 'do you feel the heat?'

'Of course. I feel heat from your hand,' she answered irritably.

He moved his hand back to an inch from her forehead and kept it hovering there. Then he touched her above the eye.

'Different energy. It has fever.'

She drew back, tired of what she considered his mumbo jumbo, tired of the searching spotlight of his eyes, and he was aggrieved. He flinched at the look he thought he saw on her face.

'Zen says to enjoy your struggle. Don't take the headache. The travels weren't easy but you must enjoy your trouble on the road. Many more travels ahead of us.'

'I don't know about that.'

'You forgive me for before, don't you?'

'I feel a distance between us.' She rejoiced in the cold words. She wasn't sure what she was about to say, but she understood it was revenge, and she would have to leave it to instinct. The way he was sitting, legs tightly crossed, his arms folded around his stomach like he was a suffering avatar infuriated her. She wanted to crack him apart, expose him. 'I have no commitment to you. That is how I truly feel.'

He was aghast.

'No! Why do you have to cut the tree down now?'

'Better I tell you now before we move on from here.'

With an explosive word she could not catch, he put his head in his hands.

'I thought you wanted to see Asia.'

'I'm sorry. It's just I don't love you enough. It's not total. Not complete.'

'Love is never complete.'

'Perhaps.'

'So you don't love me? That means you lied before.'

'No, I meant it before.'

She felt herself a sudden liar. And her appetite for a fight was already going because she knew he'd always have the mental endurance to win. The curtains sucked in and out of the windows like a mouth was pulling them in with its breath.

'Why are you so weak?' he assailed her. 'Why are you such a coward? You're a chicken. Pew. Pew. Pew,' he imitated.

'Stop that!'

'Oh, I told you too much!' he said, raising his eyes to the ceiling in despair. 'Yesterday, I told you too many terrible things about my life. I have scared you. I don't want you to suffer. Please don't let it be too late.'

'It's just I can't commit to you the rest of my life.'

She felt the shift in her own position, from initial bravery to cowardice and self justification; a refuge in the pretence of being kind enough to spare his feelings when she was in reality attempting to spare her own.

'I never asked for that; just to stay with you longer. Are you god? Do you think you can predict everything?'

'No.'

'I'm sorry I've been telling you actual what I think. I know it's my bad character. It must be disgusting to you. So, I ask you again, straight. Will you come to Asia with me?'

'I want to come.' She felt the lie in her own words.

'I want to.' He lingered distrustfully on each syllable. 'Does that mean you will?'

'Yes. But please don't ask me to promise anything.' She couldn't bear his gaze.

'I won't. Do you trust me?'

'Yes.'

'I trust you now,' he said, his straight back relaxing. He stood up and walked over to the desk, opening his notebook. 'I think sometimes we argue because I have bad English. It is my fault.' He pursed his lips. 'I promise I will try harder.'

She thought of Cambodia, but instead an image came of her own country with green fields and wild-berried hedgerows and rain that hid the hills behind its white screen only to lift suddenly like a lid, refreshed and wide awake. She thought of her parents and her homecoming, but little joy came to mind. She knew very few people there now as she'd been away a long time. She imagined wanting to visit the mother of her best friend at school, ostensibly to ask about her friend, but really to break down and confess her failed life and how all her early promise had materialised into a horrible waste.

Koji was writing feverishly in his notebook, breathing very deep. He stopped abruptly, counting on his fingers, and it seemed to her like the holy signs of a priest caught in momentary imprecation. He closed the notebook and sighed without looking at her. He never wrote for long and she understood he'd had so many painful experiences he found it difficult to write. That was why he favoured taking photos, each picture pure in the moment, blotting out the past.

'I don't want us to feel repentance, remorse or penitence,' he said, breaking the silence.

His words surprised her, then she realised he had the dictionary open beside him.

'That was what I felt being married to my wife. Repentance.'

He got up, went to the drawer and took out two aspirins, swallowing them with the dregs of the cold tea. He stood for a moment with his eyes closed. To her, he became the statue of a monk with his raised profile, bulbous eyes of uncoloured marble and thin mouth.

Nobody could imagine, she thought, the physical fear she felt with him. That was how it was with many hostages, she'd heard. It was even acknowledged as a special syndrome. Hostages could end up falling in love with their captors.

Koji returned to his desk and soon began the flick, flick of the cloth on the camera.

THE AIRPORT GAME

1

Niall glanced at his watch and cursed at the line of stationary traffic ahead. Christ, Christ, Christ. He was late to pick up Hannah from Dublin Airport and it was his own fault for stopping off at the lab on the way. He kept dreaming of her face lighting up to see his. A girlfriend had cheated on him some years ago, and it had devastated him. Through Hannah he'd got his trust back. It sounded mad but when she was far away he loved her the most; distance helped reinforce those feelings of trust.

He put the gear in neutral and it sparked off a recent memory. He'd been telling her about the time (long before their own relationship, needless to say) that he'd picked up a female hitchhiker on the way to Cork, and they'd got on so well together they ended up pulling into a lay-by and having sex in his car. Hannah had been shocked; intrigued more about the hitchhiker than the sex. Did the hitchhiker initiate it, she'd asked? He went on to tell Hannah that the sex was exciting but uncomfortable (he threw in the uncomfortable bit just so she wouldn't think he was hinting at wanting car sex) because the gearstick had been in the way, when she promptly asked if the hitchhiker had jumped on the gearstick. Her question had surprised him at the time but he'd joked it off with silly innuendo about 'the horn' and 'a full tank'. Ok, so he'd been showing off a bit, airing his bravado, but she'd wrong-footed him. He'd expected, well, he hadn't thought what he'd expected, perhaps just silence. Certainly not this implication that the sex-in-a-car girl would prefer to throw herself on the gearstick than on him.

True enough, he shouldn't have told her the story, in fact why had he in the first place? Now he thought about it, it was his own subconscious attempt to urge her to be sexually freer with him. It was a way of telling her other women found him desirable, so why didn't she? And she had insinuated that the gearstick was probably a better shag than he was. He hadn't really picked up on it at the time; he'd taken it as a kind of playful remark, but now it struck him with pain what she'd meant.

Good, the traffic ahead was starting to move. He dismissed the whole conversation – he was reading far too much into it. He thought of Hannah's body, the light shiver down her throat when she laughed. He'd be with her so soon he was starting to ache. There was always this adrenaline rush before seeing her. She was flying back from London where she'd been staying with friends.

He noticed in a car next to him, a child wearing a fleece with the words 'choose your own destiny' written all over it. 'Choose your own bullshit' he grinned to himself.

The car behind him tooted. He gripped the stick in the palm of his hand and moved into first gear.

2

Hannah arrived off the London plane on time and, on stepping into the arrivals foyer, looked round, confident of meeting her boyfriend's warm eyes, only to be met by those of strangers. When she phoned him it went straight to voicemail. A brief flare of anger was followed by worry, worry he'd had an accident, then an even greater worry he'd decided to dump her.

Not that that was possible. Niall was in love with her, and everything was cool. Only the week before she'd been telling him about her friend falling pregnant and what a nightmare it was. 'Oh, it wouldn't be so bad,' he'd said, patting her stomach. His act of tenderness had taken her by surprise; it was a future promise. She hadn't been out with many men but she felt so secure with him. Yes, it was going great. Nearly, she corrected herself. The one area of anxiety was in bed. Sex with Niall dissatisfied her and it seemed to stem from the fact he had been her first and wanted to be her last. She was almost jealous he'd had the pleasure of being the first. She also minded that, at three years older, he flaunted his past experiences over her.

Oh, he couldn't be more loving, more gentle, but every night was a shy re-enactment of the first night, with neither daring to take it on further. She resented his awe of her, but was afraid at the same time if she showed she was sexually into him she might lose his respect. There was a sense in which he jumped to her coldness, and she wasn't prepared to risk her position and power.

But the real worry was he loved her for a purity which was predicated on a lie. She knew well from her own fantasies she was anything but pure (the purity being that she'd indulged only in oral sex in her teens rather than intercourse). She understood Niall had been damaged and that she was the cure, and she was happy to be that cure, yet she felt trapped by him. His worship of her had the obverse effect of dragging her sense of her own body into a thing of baseness ...

No, she didn't want to obsess about it. She went through to the packed airport bar and took a coffee. Then she walked over to a tall table at the window and sat down, looking out for him. But she found herself gazing back towards the bar, drawn to its fast-moving, transitory bustle.

She thought again of Niall. He worked in the university as a biologist – the word itself evoked an animalistic sexuality; sniggers from the back of the dirty-minded fourth form. She wondered if it was being a scientist that made him so methodical in bed, gave a predictability to this repeated experiment – grinding her with his pestle on the mortar of the bed! She laughed at the idea. But it was her fault too, as she put him down, never gave him credit for his attractiveness.

She looked around. She was still on her holidays. She reminded herself she didn't have to go back to work till the next day. Above the bar a digital strip informed her 'Los Angeles, 06.00, 18 degrees ... Bangkok, 08.00, 25 degrees ...' Different cities, different weather, varying times, the world was on the move. All around her people were passing in their summer clothes and her mood began to rise.

She worked in a small office in a crumbling Georgian building in Dublin sub-editing a lifestyle magazine. She'd meant it to be her stepping stone into journalism and writing fiction but the job wasn't remotely creative. One of her roles was editor of the letters page and she was tired of the amusing malapropisms of readers' children and the antics of their anthropomorphic pets. Recently she'd got into trouble for deleting readers' letters and composing her own wittier versions out of sheer boredom.

She overheard a man talking to someone at the bar. 'The best thing about Ireland is you can buy odd socks here. Belter. Honest, mate, one green, one orange, you can buy them anywhere.' She listened to this outrageous assertion with interest. The guy had a confident if overenthusiastic bonhomie. He was sharply dressed, had a London accent and a gelled haircut, and there was *something about him*.

Conversation finished, he strode up to her table, Guinness in hand, and picked up the pack of cigarettes lying there. 'That's mine. Always mark my spot with it,' he said, sitting opposite her. 'D'you mind?'

'Course not. Go ahead.'

She'd seen the box of cigarettes lying there and had assumed it was empty. She hadn't realised it was a ruse. Now she looked at him, he had a cute, raffish smile. She was on holiday and she was ready for an adventure.

3

Niall ran through the domestic arrivals, listening to the message on his phone. The tailback outside the airport had made him late and he'd just realised his phone was switched off.

'Niall, I'm in the bar waiting for you. Have you got the wrong day?'

Her voice sounded snippy to his ears. He eyed the flowers in the shop, but rushed on. The bar was packed and he couldn't pick her out at first.

Ah, there she was by the window. Instead of running up and saying he was sorry, he hesitated. There was something relaxed about her, she had a half-full drink in front of her, gin and tonic by the looks of it. There was a vibe propelling him to act in a playful way.

'Can I join you?' he said coolly, sitting down opposite her.

'Go ahead,' she said, equally as coolly as she would to a stranger.

'So, are you waiting for a plane?'

'Yeah, I'm off to Peru today.'

'Oh. Sounds cool.'

'Yeah, I'm going to chill out in an Andean village for a

few weeks and get off my head on peyote, as it happens. And you?'

Niall grinned. There weren't many laughs to be had in the lab these days. His job was about finding solutions, publishing verified figures. There was no place in that world for the unknown, and a bit of crazy spontaneity was just what he needed.

'Just wait,' he said. 'I'll swing up to the bar and score us some drinks.'

4

Hannah was relieved Niall had arrived while she was sitting alone. The guy, Aidan, had left the terminal for a cigarette. She'd been flirting openly with him, and it struck her as odd how Niall had played the stranger too as soon as he'd seen her. Although it excited her she couldn't help feeling scared that Niall had been watching her and knew she was flirting with another man.

Aidan had told her he'd arrived in Ireland for his granny's funeral that morning and was waiting for his brother-in-law to pick him up from the airport. Hannah wasn't sure if any of this was true, but he didn't seem remotely put out that his lift hadn't showed and she decided to act in exactly the same way. She told him she was off to Peru, enjoying the lie because it was irrelevant, and lying struck her as a fun way to pass an afternoon in an airport. Even the *air* in airport suggested a wonderful lightness, a liberation. When Aidan had offered her a drink she'd thought, sure, why not. Three gin and tonics later he was beginning to turn her on. The potential of sex with him was starting to both thrill and frighten her and fill her with guilt. It was just as well Niall had turned up and she could transfer her playfulness to him.

'So where is it you're off to yourself?' she asked Niall as he sat back down with his pint.

'I'm off to a convention in New York. Of male gigolos.'

'Are you one of the gigolos yourself, or are you just reporting on it?'

Niall coloured with irritation.

'Why? Don't you think I could pass as a gigolo?' he retorted, stepping out of his role.

'No, of course I believe you,' she said to cover up her gaffe. 'You look pretty hot.'

'So do you. I find you beautiful.'

She basked for a moment in his compliment.

'So, both of us at the opposite ends of the hemisphere. What a pity.'

'What a pity ... but what if I asked you to finish your drink, ditch your flight to Peru and come back with me now.'

Hannah felt annoyed at the game being brought to a close so soon. Flirtiness, play, these were the things their relationship lacked. She was enjoying this feeling of being free, the sensation that she was equally capable of having sex in a car, one night stands, wild hook ups. It was a cruel irony. She'd waited to have sex with someone she loved so it would be a pure and special thing. In that way she'd condemned herself to a life similar to that of a mortal in a Greek myth, tortured by the gods into being able to eat only the same meal every day, to watch the same view, to feel the same emotion ...

She was only twenty one, her path lay mapped out for her, and she couldn't pull out because Niall was her soulmate and she loved him wholly (the problem being she hadn't tasted life wholly), but today the path had led her to the airport, a thoroughfare of ends and beginnings, and strangely it had taken on a figurative sense in that it was a place of departure.

'I didn't tell you,' she said, trying to swallow down an urge to be cruel. 'I'm actually here with my lover.'

5

'This is Niall.'

'Good to meet you,' said Niall, his voice thick with awkwardness.

Moments before, Niall had been a little turned on by the notion of what he assumed was a fantasy lover. Of course, he had to rise above feelings of jealousy but, once he'd relaxed, he began to enjoy the ride. With Aidan's flesh and blood arrival, he nearly fell off his seat. The game clicked into a higher gear. He held it together. She wanted to play, well, he'd show her. A fucking lover. But he should have realised from the beginning she was way too chilled to be sitting on her own. It struck him – this is how Hannah would look if she was cheating on him. Alive and pink-cheeked. And *hot*.

'So where are you headed?' Aidan asked Niall.

'I'm off to New York on the six o'clock.'

'Strange us here like this, us three,' said Hannah. 'A chance meeting.'

'*A Brief Encounter*,' said Aidan. 'Cracking film.'

'Except they were in a train station.'

'Yeah,' said Aidan, 'but they still did it.'

'They never did!'

'Yes, they did. Celia whassername and Trevor Howard did it alright. It was just glossed over in the film.'

'They didn't!'

'But this is us.' He looked into her eyes and added 'we could do it.'

Hannah looked briefly towards Niall.

'Sorry, mate,' said Aidan.

'No, no,' replied Niall stiffly. 'It's sound. We're all open adults.'

'Exactly. Any place, any where, any how,' said Hannah

frivolously. 'It's a question of freedom. Of seizing the day. In parks, on the back of a bus, in *cars*.'

Niall darkened. So it was his tale of car sex that was inspiring this little act. He looked at the teasing sensuality in her eyes, and hated her. This is what he'd wanted her to be like alone for him in bed, and here she was turning it on in front of a stranger. He was on the outside watching her. He had a disembodied sense of distance, as though he was just a bit player in a strange drama beyond his control. It was Hannah's game now.

For the first time in her life, Hannah felt her own power. She was making herself dance on her own strings; she was buzzing, triumphant. She was perfectly well aware of the absurdity of the situation, but it thrilled her to use her own sexuality as a plaything, just as the unknown hitchhiker had done. She noticed Niall's hand tighten on his glass and she felt no compunction. Sometimes, she hated his nurturer's hands with their soft palms and oval nails. For a second, she stepped out of the game and saw them as the hands, not of a stranger, but of someone too close to her, a captor, suffocating and claustrophobic.

'Great,' said Aidan. 'You know, I really think this is going to happen, you and me.'

'Is it now?'

She was back to being the traveller, the woman without a destination. Nothing was forbidden.

'It's my round,' she told them. 'Let me.'

As she got up from the table, Aidan looked at her breasts. Quickly, but nevertheless it was a look. As she walked away, her back straightened, suddenly snapping into a position of pride and self-awareness. Until now she'd never been able to get rid of the fourteen-year-old girl inside herself who'd been ashamed of her tiny breasts, while all around her those of her peers were expanding with voluptuous exhibitionism.

Niall had never really looked at her breasts; instead he scoured her face for its pure love. For him her breasts were small and not that important, which had hurt her, but in Aidan's eyes they not only existed but were admired. Aidan, no, the whole world was waking up to her, and it was time Niall switched on.

6

Niall kept looking over at Hannah as he chatted to Aidan. He was just about to come clean about being her boyfriend when Aidan got up to help her with the drinks. Niall was relieved in a way. It was time to finish this game, and yet he was intrigued to know how far she would go. He was watching this show with horror, but he had to admit to himself he was split between desire for Hannah and the fear of losing her.

She gazed back at him from the bar, searching for reassurance, but he turned away, his mind hardening. When he looked back at her, he no longer saw her. It was mad. It was as if beneath Hannah's expression he could see the hitchhiker's. The woman he'd lusted after but had pretty much despised.

Hannah and Aidan sat back down with the drinks. Her leg banged against the table drunkenly.

'Don't you think you should cool it on the g and t?' asked Niall.

Hannah rarely drank spirits, only at parties, on exceptional occasions. This stranger was drinking gin and tonic and the stranger in her answered 'some like it cool. Some like it hot.'

'She's fine,' said Aidan. 'She's on her hols.'

'On holiday anything can happen,' she said.

'Why are you always smiling at me?' asked Aidan.

'Because I like to.'

'Have you ever done this before?'

'Done what before?'

'This.'

Aidan leant forward and she mirrored him, her lips moving forward to meet the hook of his words, conscious she had to do something, to end what she'd started, stop this feeling of dizziness, wildness, out of control ...

They kissed.

Niall got up, blindly, knocked his chair over, and stumbled away.

Hannah pulled back from the kiss. Aidan had bit her so hard it hurt. Her hand flew up to her lip in the expectation of blood. She got up quickly, knocking her drink over. It smashed on the floor.

'Sorry, sorry,' she said and started to run after Niall. 'Wait!' she cried out, but he wouldn't stop. She tried to cling on to his arm, but he pushed her away. She ran in front of him, blocking his way.

'Whore, whore, whore ...' he kept saying.

There was a wet hardness in his eyes she'd never seen before. She held on to him and she could smell his sweat through his shirt, could feel the animal in him, and it excited her.

'Isn't it time for your flight?' he heard his own voice say without pity.

'It wasn't me in there, it wasn't me,' Hannah cried out.

Later, much later, they both lay in bed, exhausted, holding each other. They had just had cruel, impatient, clawing sex, grabbing at each other, desperate to find one another once more.

Hannah could still feel the bruise on her lip as she watched the lights of passing traffic slide evanescently across the wall. She and Niall slowly moved apart.

WHAT HAPPENED TO YOU

It's not you, Ioanna, it's Athens that's the problem. It's the place sending me crazy. It's this hot headachey city. Or is it you? There's a Greek song that goes 'who are you to come into everyone's life and change it?' You told me about it yourself, remember?

You've turned my mind to thoughts of love, thoughts that drive me mad, asleep and awake, day and night, sucking away at my mind like mosquitoes. A low streetlight hum of love I can never possess.

You say I'm like a child, though I'm nearly twenty two, that I've never experienced love, even though there's a man waiting for me back in Belfast. You ask if I think he has slept with other people, and when I say 'no way would James ever cheat' you tell me to fuck myself and call me a little innocent. You need to live, learn about people, you tell me. You make me long to have more experiences. It's like having bad eyesight and longing to see better.

'This city's killing me,' you sigh one day, looking up at the smog-infused nacreous sky.

I have a few days free from teaching, so you take me off on a sticky, leather-seated bus to the coast. It's so packed we can't get seats together, and the young guy I'm sitting next to falls asleep on my shoulder, trapping me with the weight of it, pinning me with a wrestling move, and when I flare my eyes, you frown and signal at me to make an aggressive shoulder charge. Instead I give him a few gentle bumps and his head finally flops to the other side.

The coast comes into sight, the water a dazzling dragonfly blue, relieved by a foam as white as Greek marble.

You put on your red-rimmed plastic sunglasses which are tacky in a hip cool way. We trundle our suitcases over the dusty concrete. A cotton scarf I'm wearing slips off onto the road, only for a guy on a scooter to roar over it. When I pick it up there's a stripe of black rubber tread across its white.

'Just as well your neck wasn't in it,' you laugh.

At last, we arrive at our rented apartment. A rotund Greek woman in slippers and some sort of housecoat shows us in, creaking across the floorboards with as much noise as a listing ship. You asked for a twin room but she shows us a double bed.

'No matter,' you say, grinning at me.

Everything seems a bit odd in this unfashionable yet modern apartment. The WiFi code is up on the kitchen wall in a gilt picture frame like it's an old master.

A kitten is yowling outside our door, so I bring it out some milk and give it a petting. It pirouettes ecstatically round my hand, but after a minute I tire of hunkering down.

'That's just like you,' you remark wryly. 'You wouldn't satisfy anyone for long.'

As soon as we've freshened up we go out to explore. As we pass the hedgerows you clap your hands, and when you open them you show me the butterfly, alive but prone and confused. It was a trick you learnt as a child in your mountain village, and you tell me it's important to do it softly so you don't shake the powder off their wings. I'd try too only I'm afraid of killing it.

'You're always afraid,' you smile.

After lunch we pass a children's park, and you can't resist going in and swinging your strong, small body round the metal bars. You could have been a gymnast, whereas I was so inflexible my gym teacher had to literally push me into doing a forward roll.

On the beach you strip down to your black swimsuit and I strip down to my tropical flower print bikini, steering my coconut-white body over to a sun lounger under an umbrella, while you lie in the sun a few inches away. Light and dark, dark and light.

'In your case, it's not a sun lounger but a shade lounger,' you laugh.

I keep adding more and more layers of sunblock to myself, never satisfied like an impressionist with a palette knife.

'It's an obsessive compulsive disorder,' you say, grabbing the lotion out of my hand, wanting me to swim, so I run with you into the waves and flap about in the shallows, while you strike off into the deep, your wet black bob almost phocine in the distance. I delight in lying back on the brine, leaving behind the gravity and worries of earth. I stay so long on the surface my skin is shrinking into some tiny piece of salted sundried beef, and I hurry back to the shade. Later, you run up the beach, invigorated, like you're in some audition for *Love Island*.

Back at the apartment we collapse on our bed. One of your favourite Greek films is on the TV. You curl right up into me and put your head on my breast. I edge back a little, and you say I'm cold.

'Go on, come closer,' you urge. 'I'm not a ghost.'

The trouble is you confuse me and it's only because of the heat I feel for you I make myself cold. Little by little, I'm starting not to trust myself anymore.

As the sun descends, we shower the salt sea off us. Our hair's wet, but we don't have time to dry it as you're starving, having swum half the Aegean. You put on a white shirt. It's your habit to wear either black shirts or white shirts, no colours, as if in your own fascistic army. The sun has warmed your tawny skin, lighting up your odalisque eyes. You always wear too much red lipstick with no other makeup, which is either garish or striking, I can't make my mind up.

When I look in the mirror my nose has turned pink, and I'm furious with myself for lying too long in the sea. You find my nose highly amusing, call me 'my little freak', then kiss the tip of it which you say you only do for special friends. I'm not at all confident about my looks, but pat a bit of powder on my face and out we go to dinner.

Later we find a pub, auspiciously called 'Making Friends Bar', but there's hardly a chance of meeting anyone because it's early June and not yet high season. We sit at the bar and flirt with the barmen, but they're looking at you all the time, not me. A quick trip to the bathroom reveals that my red hair is frizzed out in an Afro with sun and salt damage – only the zap of a hairdryer could have saved it. I return to the bar, a bit rankled that you on the other hand still have your impeccably straight black bob.

The handsome bartender keeps bestowing free drinks on us as I chat listlessly to his plainer sidekick who has an alarming scar round his neck that makes him look like he's been garotted.

'Where are you from?' the garotted one asks.

'Northern Ireland,' I say, and he shakes his head because he knows, he has maps in his mind of how women from all parts of Europe are, and he thinks I'm a puritan and wishes I was German.

Suddenly I'm dying to get back to the bars of Athens where the men try to make me love them; men who whisper that even if I leave them, they'll always be dancing in my mind.

Eventually, you say it's time to go. On the way back to our apartment you tell me the bartender said 'what are you bothering with her for? Look at her and look at you.'

'Thanks a lot,' I say.

The sea with its sibilant slurs sounds almost sloshed.

The following morning the first thing I'm aware of is you opening the blinds. The room fills with a heavenly sunshine. The next thing I'm aware of is an itch on my hand and more on my arms and legs. One quick scratch and the bites are up like boils. I look like I've succumbed to the bubonic plague.

'You should be flattered. Mosquitoes only go for the sweetest blood,' you say, assuaging my irritation with a mollifying smile.

You anoint me with Sudocrem and show me the one miniscule mosquito bite on your arm. You're nearly immune to them yourself. The hot night has made my skin sweat and the eczema rage in my ear. To add insult to injury there's dermatitis on my wrist from the nickel on my watch.

You go rummage in the kitchen and bring out some extra virgin olive oil.

'Extra virgin,' you laugh as you dab it on my wrist. 'This is the only part of you that is!'

I look out ruefully at the swampy pond to the back of the apartments, the home of flying, nibbling creatures.

Surely if my body's going to be feasted on it should be by a man rather than a mosquito.

We head out for lunch. The sun beats down and I wish I had a portable parasol with me like a Victorian heroine. The motorbike-print scarf is wrapped round my head and I'm horribly aware of huge polka dots of Sudocrem on my legs.

Later, you drag me off to the beach where I sit in the shade reading Solzhenitsyn's *Cancer Ward*, smoking a cigarette. I don't feel so bad about the cigarette as at least I'm avoiding skin cancer under the umbrella, but you rib me for my 'light holiday reading' before heading off into the lambent blue sea.

I try to write an email to James on my phone but how can I tell him how my life is with you, about the pubs we visit, the men we talk to. I'm afraid he'll see the danger behind everything I say. He knows me, he'll guess what's happening to me, be able to tell my resistances are weakening. All that can save me is my flight home in three weeks' time, but even that's too late. Because my senses have been awakened forever.

It's happening to all of us teachers over here. One teacher tried to seduce one of the other female teachers who's married. It's this city, it's this city, though it's you too. Sometimes you see the effect the men here are having on me, arousing me almost to breaking point and you look at my dazed expression and say 'what happened to you?'

You pad up the beach quickly to avoid the heat of the sand on your soles, then stand over me, shaking the water out of your hair, deliberately splashing me.

'You Irish miss the rain,' you tease.

You sit down cross-legged on your towel and let the sand filter through your two fists, connecting like an hour glass. Then you start reading *Lolita*.

'By the way,' you say, looking provocatively over your sunglasses. 'I'm still waiting for you to seduce Dimitris Savlopoulos.'

Dimitris Savlopoulos is one of my pupils.

'He's only thirteen,' I protest.

'So? He's beautiful.'

He's the principal's son, a blond Greek, irresistibly golden haired with a golden tan. I've been ice skating with him and I've taken him for ice cream, all in the name of improving his conversational English, but his father would die if he knew what particular education you had in mind.

The glare of the sun on the white sand is too much and I go back to the apartment for a lie down, covering myself with the sheet to keep out the mosquitoes. I dream lightly you're making my bed for me, so it'll be nice for a man to come and sleep in. Then I feel a sharp pain in my head and wake up.

'Sorry,' you say, hovering above me, 'but there's a mosquito in your hair.'

You pull again, laughingly showing me a hair you've just yanked out.

'Cut it out!' I yell.

Then you begin to tickle me and I wriggle away to the other side of the bed.

'Why don't you kick me out?' you ask puzzled.

But I don't want you to leave and, when you finally do, I move over to where the warmth of your body lingers.

It's getting dark and the night opera of the cicadas is preluding louder and louder.

I shower and blow-dry my hair, but I'm still a white shadow of myself. You on the other hand are glowing, and the hagiographer of the sun has blessed your beautiful skin. You are the anointed one and I'm the ointmented one. I wear a long-sleeved shirt to hide my bites.

Outside, the air reminds me of a woman who's sprayed herself with scent on a night out. We breathe in the jasmine growing up the walls; the thyme, myrtle and sage from the restaurant gardens.

We return to the pub of last night's flirtation where the bartender stares into your eyes, lavishing drinks on us. Even though his English is perfectly good, you exclude me by chatting away in Greek. I manage to sidestep the attentions of the garotted barman by excusing myself and going to the bathroom. In the mirrors, I notice my nose is peeling worse than a damp Belfast wall and has now progressed into a pink and white blotch. It really isn't fair, especially as if we were in Belfast I would be radiantly white, whereas you'd have that slightly sallow, jaundiced look that afflicts Mediterranean skin types under our dark sky.

When I re-emerge, a handsome Greek man starts chatting to me in spite of my leprous nose, and I find out he works for a homeless charity which no doubt explains why he's so kind to me.

'Travel is the ... the essence of life,' he says, rubbing his thumb against his fingers, searching for the right words, like he's crumbling soil onto a grave.

His hair is shaved short, and I long to run my fingers over the stipplings of tiny black spikes. His head reminds me of a sea urchin. It feels like there are sexual signals between us, smiles and nods and eye flares, but they keep moving in and out of distance.

Soon you get jealous and come to spirit me away. As I knew all along you've no use for the bartender. He's far too keen, and you're only in love with men who don't love you like Mahis back in Athens; men whose hearts are broken. You told me the story of how you fell in love with Mahis yourself, when one night you noticed this girl singing to him really passionately while he waved her away, numb in the sadness of his own lost love. You probably should have taken it as a sign he wouldn't be interested in you either, but you love a lost cause and that's just the way you are with your love of the unattainable, the unpossessable.

On the walk home, you take off your ring and pass it to me.

'Here. I want you to wear this forever.'

It's the ring your boyfriend gave you, the one you were going to marry.

'I can't. It belongs to you,' I protest, but you seize my right hand, slipping it on to my finger. In Greece married couples often wear their rings on their right hand, and I can't help feeling you're making me yours.

Back at the apartment we get into bed together, face to face.

You kiss me tenderly.

'I'm going to miss you so much. How long is it till you leave?'

'Three weeks,' I say.

'In three weeks you'll step off the plane and say to James, "Take me to your bed." Lucky you!'

I turn away. You tap me on the shoulder but I don't look back. I long to tell you I'm in the only bed I want. Tears prickle in my eyes and I'm scared you'll see.

'You won't look at me,' you say. 'God, you're so strange sometimes. So cold.'

Then you turn the opposite way and fall asleep.

In the morning, you bounce out of bed early.

'Let's go back to Athens. I hate the sea.'

'Are you sure?' I check, scratching two new mozzie bites. My nose has faded, making the bites the only bit of colour on me. Two days at the beach and I still have the pallor of Greek yoghurt; my legs are paler than feta!

You're adamant about leaving and what you say goes, as I know you're far stronger than me. Even though I'm bigger, if we stood opposite and threw rocks at each other I'd be the first to fall.

Part of me wants to stay marooned with you in the apartment, but the bright light of the electric blue sea is hurting my eyes. It's hard to live in this brash 3D neon world, and so we pack quickly and head back to Athens on the bus. We're sitting next to a middle-aged Irish couple who keep trying to outdo each other in garnering attention. The woman yawns out a series of truncated notes in an ostentatious aria of exhaustion propelling you to roll your eyes at me. There's nothing like travelling alongside my own nationality to make me realise how much I hate them. At least it feels good to be shuttling back to the shady nuances of the city, back to the sky as cloudy white as ouzo.

Your sister has come to pick us up in her car and the second you see her you kiss her really passionately on the lips. It confuses me. I don't know how things are anymore.

I instantly feel better as soon as I swap sun for smog and my skin starts to heal. It transpires that unhealthy environments are actually healthy for me. Cicadas are replaced by the hum of traffic and the buzz of the aircon. I can hear phones, televisions and the shouting that to Greeks is normal conversation. I go back to my classes.

The evening after our return I'm due to take Dimitris to the cinema, but Mr Savlopoulos cancels the arrangement at the last minute saying 'on second thoughts, I don't think Dimitris should stay out so late.' With me, he means. Even my boss can see what Greece is doing to me, what is happening to me. Everyone can see the danger lapping higher and higher.

I've only two weekends left before I go back to James. The one mirror that always tells me I'm beautiful is the one in his eyes, but the trouble is I've learnt the pain and pleasure of loving without hope, and I'm not sure I'm any good for him now. They say living in a city makes you feel empty, but I'm full of wistful longing. I vow to myself to find a man, to sate myself before I have to leave. The danger's so close it's touching my skin and it's like water on hot streets.

One Friday night I'll go out with you and I'll find a man who loves the moon, who says those born on the full moon can see things in the trees and skies; a man who whispers his mystic beliefs, holds me, says he must have me; a man who sings to me that Greek song that goes 'just give me one night, one night, goodnight, goodnight ...'

I lie and rest on my bed, but the sheets start to move around me, sliding up and down my skin, and someone is inside the bed with me. Shhhh. No, it isn't real, it isn't real. It's the breeze from the balcony.

On Friday morning, however, my plan falls apart – I wake up earlier than usual with a jolt, itching all over. I walk into the bathroom and see these huge circles of pixelated pink on my legs, torso and arms; a red epicentre surrounded by rose rings. Picking up my iPad in a panic, I start googling. From the images it looks to be ticks or ringworm, or perhaps I'm the victim of some rare form of biological warfare. Oh god, it occurs to me it must have been from cuddling that fucking kitten on the coast.

I phone Mr Savlopoulos who asks his brother-in-law doctor to make a house visit. I understand from the doctor's broken English/sign language mash up that it's definitely ringworm, it's going to take two to four weeks to heal, and until then I'll be contagious. He leaves me a large tub of cream with which I douse myself.

Later, I run round to your apartment and tell you what's up with me, explaining I can't go out tonight.

'Oh, no,' you exclaim. 'It means I can't even kiss you before you leave Athens.'

'I know,' I say, imagining your red lips on me and your soft embraces.

I walk back home along the crumbling pavements under the hot, hazy sky. There's a strange liquidity in the air that makes everything seem on the verge of dissolution, but it may just be the fever. All I keep seeing is an image of myself as a butterfly in your hands, the flaky, salt powder shaken off my wings.

Rosemary Jenkinson is a playwright and short story writer from Belfast. She taught English in Greece, France, the Czech Republic and Poland before returning to Belfast in 2002. Her plays include *The Bonefire* (Stewart Parker BBC Radio Award), *Planet Belfast*, *Here Comes the Night*, *Michelle and Arlene*, *May the Road Rise Up* and *Lives in Translation*. Her plays have been performed in Dublin, Belfast, London, Edinburgh, Brussels, Melbourne, Washington DC and New York. She was 2017 artist-in-residence at the Lyric Theatre in Belfast, and in 2018 she received a Major Artist Award from the Arts Council of Northern Ireland.

Rosemary's short story collections are *Contemporary Problems Nos. 53 & 54*, *Aphrodite's Kiss*, *Catholic Boy* (shortlisted for the EU Prize for Literature), and *Lifestyle Choice 10mgs* (shortlisted for the Edge Hill Short Story Prize). She was singled out by the *Irish Times* for 'an elegant wit, terrific characterisation and an absolute sense of her own particular Belfast'.

She was writer-in-residence at the Leuven Centre for Irish Studies in 2019.